In League with a UFO

Second Edition

In League with a UFO

Second Edition

By

Lou Baldin

In League with a UFO

Published through Lulu Enterprises, Inc.

Copyright © 1997 1ST edition, by Lou Baldin

Copyright © 2009 2nd edition, by Lou Baldin

Second Edition.

ISBN: 978-0-578-01330-5

Contents

Prologue

T he flying disk recovered in Roswell, New Mexico, in 1947 is one of many contacts with extraterrestrial life forms humans have had in the last century, and this new century. Roswell received the bulk of the interest because personnel in the United States government inadvertently reported it to a worldwide audience. Days after an officer from the military released the news that an Alien ship had crashed in a field near Roswell, New Mexico, a substantial amount of repudiation of the story poured out from military headquarters debunking the original account. However, not everyone could be silenced. For some of the individuals, those that experienced the phenomena firsthand, the cover-up did not alleviate their new paranormal realities. During that period many of the people touched by the extraterrestrial affair such as nurses, doctors, scientists, and military personnel, the people with firsthand knowledge, suddenly lost interest in telling their stories. Those people had been debriefed on the consequences should they talk about what they saw and experienced in Roswell.

Much of what leaked out in the last three decades came from people that had previously sworn secrecy about their involvement while employed by the newly developed covert society. These people lived most of their lives working in clandestine laboratories setup in several places around the world. Some of the scientists in those programs had physical contact with extraterrestrials and their magical technologies salvaged from the Alien ship at Roswell. A few of those people eventually wrote books describing some of the things they worked around, but for the fantastic nature of their claims, fewer people believed them. Others, with more profound information and fearful of losing credibility, careers, and even their life, had no interest in going public. Some remained quiet out of duty to country. Most of these people have gone to their graves, taking their secrets with them. However, not all secrets went to the grave. Some remained hidden in dusty attics and damp basements, stored away under old magazines and books, in boxes, awaiting discovery. Much of that material, as is true with countless other historical documents throughout history, has been forever lost to posterity. No one will ever know how much secret information from that incident in history and other covert projects made it to the landfills, but some journals have mysteriously resurfaced after the author(s) passed away.

When I first wrote "In League with a UFO", I did not want to be associated with the UFO phenomena and was not sure how to put the information out without admitting my personal experiences in the phenomena. I put the manuscript away for two years before revisiting it again, and finally publishing the manuscript. Unbeknownst to me at the time, and coincidently I might add, my book came out in print two weeks before the fiftieth anniversary of the Roswell crash. My publisher informed me of that fact and suggested that I should take advantage of the crowds that would converge on Roswell, New Mexico on July of 1997, to sell my books. I declined, and my book remained for the most part unknown for nearly ten years after publication. A few books sold at local bookstores, and in the second year, I was invited to the filming of a documentary concerning UFOs. I attended the conference, but I did not participate in the documentary. However, I did participate in two radio interviews on a later date.

How I came to have this information is as strange as the information itself. I was a homebuilder at the time with no desire to write a book and little if any writing ability to write a book. I received a call one day and invited to have lunch by an individual I did not know. I often met with clients and suppliers in the construction fields that invited me to lunch for the purpose of sales pitches concerning new building materials. I met with this fellow at an upscale restaurant and we talked about writing books instead of construction materials. During our conversation, he handed me some papers that he took from his briefcase and showed them to me. I do not recall what we talked about or what was on those papers nor has that person ever contacted me again. However, two or three weeks after meeting that person I began to write down the material that is in this book.

UFO Crash

T he year was 1947, the place, Roswell, New Mexico. On July 2, of that year, some of the town's people made reports of a bright disk streaming across the sky to the local authorities. The unidentified flying object (UFO) fell from the sky and crashed approximately seventy-five miles northwest of town that day. A rancher, or farmer that heard the crash, thought that an airplane had fallen into a field a short distance from his house, and went to investigate. What he found at the scene was not anything he could relate to, and the object certainly did not look to him like it was from this world! He was so mystified about what he saw that he failed to report the incident until five days later, on July 7, during some other business he had to do in town. He told some friends that the craft was made of a strange material that had no weight to it, yet seemed to have incredible strength. Once the news spread about the rancher's claim of finding a UFO, the excitement, mixed with apprehension about a possible Alien invasion, spread throughout the town like brush fire. It was not long after the rancher showed the crash site to one of the military officers that the rancher abruptly became silent on the topic and spoke no more about it. He refused to discuss what he had found with the media or his friends. Nevertheless, the news was out, and it quickly traveled around the country and the world as reporters inundated that small New Mexico town.

Ironically, much of what is known concerning the UFO crash was released to the media by a public relations officer from the military, the same military that later denied the story. A military officer told the press that a flying disk had crashed and that the military had recovered the UFO. From that statement, people all over the world wanted to know more. Some of the talk around the town focused on topics that questioned the vary nature of humanity's existence. "What if we are not alone in the universe? Was the crash proof that other life forms existed? And if so, what a scary thought that was!" Those were some of the concerns brought up by the town folk.

Orson Welles' narration of *War of the Worlds,* in 1938, was fresh on the minds of many people in Roswell, and people around the country too. The alleged Alien crash implied that a real invasion from other worlds could be imminent. There was anxiety mixed with excitement about such a prospect. Those were certainly dire implications, and the government soon realized it was not in a position to answer the queries and concerns coming at them by the potentially panic provoking reporters. Not knowing what the military had in its possession, and at the same time attempting to halt what had turned into a media-circus of paranoia, the military retracted its earlier statement about a flying disk, blaming the misunderstanding on a misinformed lower ranking officer. The military's updated report simply stated that a new kind of weather balloon tested in the nearby military base is what they recovered from the now famous Roswell crash. The crash of a weather balloon was easier to swallow than alleged Aliens from space, and a lot less frightening for the public at large. Few people doubted the military's revised explanations and welcomed them, and the public quickly forgot the whole matter.

Cover-Up

T he top brass in the military establishment was unable to give the President of the United States pertinent details of what they had in their possession, other than the ship appeared to be extraterrestrial and not of this world. That was enough information for the President to make the decision to keep the whole affair a secret, until further notice.

A secret committee convened with the sole purpose of studying the Alien ship. The committee, under the jurisdiction of the Air Force, received its funding from them. The committee operated under the pretext of integrating new technologies for the development of superior maneuverability and faster flying military aircraft. The facility was located near the Nevada-Arizona border and popularly known as "Area 51." The base was one of the most hush-hush bases in the country until sometime in the Nineteen Seventies. That is when UFO buffs began mentioning the secret base in their meetings, and the media began writing about the secret base in newspapers and magazines.

Information about UFOs came from a multitude of sources. From the average citizen that reported to the media that they had seen aircraft perform fantastic feats of maneuverability near and around military bases, and from professionals, that claimed what they saw defied all concepts of what military aircraft, or any human constructed aircraft, was capable of, without breaking apart. Moving diagonally while traveling at a high rate of speed was one of the more bizarre instances reported. Other sources or leaks came from former military personnel that worked at certain bases and spoke under the condition that their identities would remain hidden. Area 51 remains a top-secret facility, but everyone knows its whereabouts now. The base serves more as a decoy, keeping the public focused on it and away from other concealed operations across the country, according to a document.

The military had in its possession a flying machine so advanced and mysterious that some of the scientists involved in the program speculated that it could only be from other dimensions. The Alien ship was capable of traveling from one dimension to another, as a means to traverse the vastness of space inside our Milky Way galaxy. "The ship was like a living organism," claimed a document in one of the secret files. When recovered, the ship had a large hole on one side of it. At first, the committee believed that the ship exploded due to a leaky antimatter type component in the ship. The explosion annihilated a large portion of the ship (the actual size of the Alien ship was missing from the documents). Miraculously, three weeks after the craft's discovery, the ship completely healed (repaired) itself. To say the least, it was a very mysterious event, since the committee monitored the ship twenty-four hours a day, and no Alien work crew materialized to perform the work. If Aliens did repair the ship, they were invisible, or the Aliens rendered the guards unconscious and implanted false memories into their minds. The scientists that monitored the ship reported that the healing of the ship occurred similar to a human flesh wound. The skin or surface of the ship simply grew back over a period of days. In realty, there is no similarity to the human immunology and that of the ship's own ability to heal. Had a human suffered an equivalent trauma as the ship had, nothing would have grown back and the human would have died. Once the ship healed, there was no sign of the original damage.

The debris from the explosion covered several acres of land with material that had the appearance and consistency of aluminum foil, except that aluminum foil remains crumpled when crumpled and easily damaged. The Alien material bounced back without a wrinkle and appeared to be indestructible. Since the ship repaired itself, the scientists investigating the ship were unable to determine the cause of the crash. After further studies of the material and its strength, the scientists concluded that nothing earthly could have harmed the ship in anyway, nor caused the slightest damage to it, including a lighting strike (one of the original theories on what caused the saucer to crash).

Of the three Aliens recovered from the craft, one was dead and two were alive. The three Aliens removed from the ship at the time of its recovery were taken to an undisclosed location away from the ship. The secret committee in possession of the ship had no knowledge of the whereabouts of the beings once "other people" removed the Aliens. At that time, the committee was unconcerned about the Alien beings. The committee members had plenty on their plate with the ship and the mysterious cargo living in it!

Several months passed before the scientists felt somewhat comfortable working inside of the ship. Entering the ship was as if walking into a time warp, all sense of reality instantly vanished. Wristwatches did not function inside the Alien ship, and neither did the five human senses. Things smelled differently or not at all while in the ship. Body odor lost its pungency. However, the food they brought into the ship for experimental purposes, gave off offensive smells, as if the food became rancid. Perfume and cologne were undetectable until the scientists stepped out of the ship and their noses once again adjusted to the scent.

From the experiments with food, the scientists determined that the food was not permanently affected or altered, and the food regained the natural smell and taste when it was taken out of the ship. The other senses: sight, hearing, and touch, changed for the better. If a certain scientist wore glasses, he needed to remove them to see. It was the same with hearing. All sound was clear regardless of previous hearing abilities. Touch was sensitive to the point of being erotic. The ship simply felt good! However, the scientists were not accustomed to feeling optimally good and healthy, and it took time (most never did) before they became comfortable with the invigorating sensations inside the ship's environment. When the scientists spent long periods in the ship, coming out of the ship was akin to severe jetlag, they became irritable, groggy, drained, achy, and needed time to readjust to feeling lousy again. Ironically, feeling lousy was the normal feeling of their bodies they had forgotten about while in the ship.

Although the senses were on high alert while in the ship, the description that was unanimous among those that entered the ship was that it was surreal. They were in a dreamy state of mind, yet, they were energized and not at all drowsy while in the ship. However, that state of clarity turned into apprehension, and for some, nightmarish. The persistent feeling that something living (extraterrestrial) was present in the ship with them, behind them, around them, like wisps or shadows that never quite came into focus, gnawed at them. The unknown elements of the ship were unnerving for those working inside the ship. No doubts in the minds of the scientists that they were not alone while in the ship, regardless the fact that the three beings had been removed from it!

To compensate for the time distortion while in the ship the scientists posted sentries outside the ship and had one of them enter the ship every few minutes to announce the time to those inside. When first discovered, the scientists spent hours and sometimes days inside the ship, oblivious to the fact that even a single minute had passed. Sometimes it was the opposite, and it seem like they spent an eternity inside the ship when only a few minutes passed. Working long stretches of time without losing energy or focus was common and addictive, and created havoc for those with families.

The interior of the craft was much larger than its physical exterior suggested. No one was sure whether all the rooms and compartments on the ship were discovered. Everyone that entered the ship came out with different numbers of rooms. Even the same individual would come out with a different number each time he left the craft. Another problem the scientists faced was leaving the ship with intelligible notes. Everything they wrote down ended up being a maze of half-written words and sentences void of meaning once they exited the ship. The scientists attempted to take pictures of the instruments and other interior rooms of the ship, but were unsuccessful. When the film was developed, it was as if it had been exposed to light. They tried different systems of shielding the camera from the unknown radiation. They enclosed the camera in various alloys, plastics, and exotic cutting-edge ceramics, in hopeless attempts to insulate the film. Nothing worked.

The ship contained numerous gadgets. Some of the gadgets were removed from the ship during experimentations with them. Some gadgets, even though they were portable while in the ship, could not be taken out of the ship. An invisible force field inside the ship stopped the scientists from leaving the ship with certain Alien gadgets. No one was able to figure out how to circumvent the force.

Alien gadgets somehow knew what their purpose was. Unlike human gadgets such as hammers and toasters, which required human input to function, or an electrical outlet, Alien gadgets had an independent life of their own. Alien gadgets appeared to have consciousness (they were alive), and performed duties independently and without any known power source such as batteries, solar cells, electrical cords, and operated indefinitely!

The opening or doorway into the Alien ship was another mystery. When a scientist approached the craft with the intention of entering it, an opening appeared instantly. If there was no intention by the scientist of entering the ship, nothing opened. The ship could be entered from any location, top, sides, and from the bottom of the ship. Wherever a scientist approached the ship that is where they entered. When an opening manifested it led to the same central location, regardless of the point of entry. The craft was also able to absorb several people into it at once. A feat that left many of the scientists spooked beyond comprehension. According to one testimony, "if all the technicians that were analyzing the ship formed a circle around it and intended to enter it in mass they all did!" There were no doors, as we know and understand doors, only an opening that accommodated the size of the person or persons entering the ship. The ship appeared to work something like osmosis. The person desiring entry and standing next to the ship instantly found himself or herself inside the ship. Yet, if there was no mental desire to enter or exit, the ship remained impregnable. No man-made machinery could break into the ship.

Weird and Wondrous Life Forms

E verything in the ship possessed unique personalities that were also capable, in the most bizarre ways, of conveying emotions to the scientists. The best description of these gadgets by the scientists was that they were like synthetic versions of insects and small animals. They lacked organic qualities in the respect that they did not eat, drink, or eliminate, yet the gadgets did not have inert qualities of synthetic human-made materials, either. The Alien gadgets squirmed, crawled, levitated, jumped, flew, and walked! The size of the living gadgets ranged from a deer tick, to a basketball, with the majority of the items fitting in the palm of the average person's hand. The scientists treated some gadgets as delightful toys, and occasionally fought over them like children, impatiently waiting their turn to inspect, explore, and be entertained by the gadgets. However, some of the Alien gadgets turned out to be monsters.

Many of the gadgets appeared metallic, sturdy, and unbelievably strong, and at the same time malleable, like putty. The ambiguity of the strange substance that the gadgets were made of confounded the research teams. The consensus was that the material from which the ship and its contents consisted of made a mockery of human physics. Alien gadgets did not function similarly to Earth based machinery with gears, motors, wheels, wiring, or state-of-the-art solid-state microelectronics. Nor did the gadgets function physiologically, with bone, blood, and muscle, or plant and marine life. It appeared that every molecule of whatever these things were made of acted in unison in the same manner that water molecules joined together to create ocean waves.

There were no human means available to dissect the Alien gadgets. They were impervious to our inferior technology to penetrate and analyze them. The Alien things had no seams or edges to pry open, no organs or flesh to probe; they could not be weighed, or their contents measured. They appeared cast from one solid piece with no individual parts, except that they were not solid, as we understand solid to be. One analogy describing Alien material was malleable and solid, but temperature had nothing to do with either state, as it does with Earth metals, liquids, and gases. Alien gadgets transitioned to four physical stages: solid, malleable, liquid, and gas, without external heat variation or pressure changes. Change happened at the discretion of the Alien gadget and not the human handler. Attempts to study the items were further blunted when X-ray failed to penetrate the Alien material. There was no human means to understand what made the gadgets operate other than from the paranormal.

Nothing connected with the ship aged, wore out, or became obsolete; rather, the things in the ship and the ship itself, appeared to improve over time. The gadgets also learned the habits of the handlers. An example, if a hammer were an Alien gadget, all one needed to do was use it once and from then on the hammer would repeat the action indefinitely, hitting the nail without the need to handle the hammer manually. The hammer would operate on its own, although, someone had to hold the nail and pray that the hammer did not miss. Alien technology, however perfect, is problematic when interfacing with inferior technology and lack of understanding. The scientists discovered that controlling an Alien item once it activated was a dangerous proposition. Several accidents and fatalities due to human/Alien interactions happened.

The ship had two or three rooms equipped like futuristic surgical operating rooms. The rooms were brighter and had the feeling of a place where flesh encountered scalpel. Members of the team believed that many, if not all of the gadgets on the ship, performed medical functions.

After suffering a few mishaps (loss of life and limb) from coming into direct contact with bizarrely alive Alien gadgets during experimentation on each other, the scientists decided to utilize cadavers instead of themselves in order to reduce pain, suffering, and death among its members. After many failed attempts to get the Alien gadgets to function on cadavers (the Alien gadgets did not respond to dead flesh), the scientists began using live animals such as rats, rabbits, pigs, chickens, mice, cows, horses, toads, fish, and other types of wildlife. Some Alien instruments activated (woke up), when exposed to certain animals. Cattle, horses, and humans always triggered the Alien gadgets to perform a freakish maneuver.

The Alien gadgets had no outward appearances or labeling that identified the functions associated with them. Scientists discovered what each gadget did mostly by accident. Deciphering what any gadget was capable of doing or performing was impossible using the tried-and-true methods of deduction. The scientists had to stumble around, sometimes awkwardly and maybe foolishly, until a function or procedure presented itself. Discoveries during testing happened by placing the Alien gadgets directly on the animals or in close proximity to the animals, and then a "wait-and-see" approach went into play. A response from the gadgets might take place instantly or it could take hours, and in some cases, more than a day before the gadgets decided to do something. The subjects, animal or human, were not sedated during the experiments because sedatives seemed to compromise the testing. In some cases, the Alien gadgets were fastened to the subjects with the use of straps, clamps, and tape. Holding the Alien gadget in place had its own consequences for the experimenters, sometimes the Alien gadget performed its "thing" on the person holding it, which was not a pretty picture, according to one source.

When dormant, some of the gadgets were spherical and had the appearance of black ball bearings; other gadgets strayed from the pack and changed colors while inert. Most of the items were smaller than a baseball and larger than a golf ball, but new gadgets appeared and disappeared regularly.

Touching certain items sucked the heat from the fingertips, and in some instances caused a few scientists to lose parts of their fingers from frostbite or exotic Alien radiation. At times the gadgets' physical weight (referred to as obstinacy in the documents), was such that the scientists could not pick up or move the gadgets, even with the use of machines and other leveraging devices. Other times those same immovable objects were lighter than air, and bobbed around the laboratory like helium balloons at a birthday party.

During the experiments with animals, the scientists discovered that some gadgets responded when they came within one inch from touching the animal. Other gadgets needed full contact with the animal before activating. Gadgets were deemed activated when they reacted in any number of ways, such as change color, size, or shape, or outright performed a function on the subject animal: remove a specific body part or perform a biopsy, or any number of strange transactions that the scientists did not fully comprehend. What the Alien instruments did was unclear with the early experimenters. In some of the early notes that survived were statements that the Alien objects mutilated the animals by removing tissue and sometimes organs from them for no apparent reason. The animals were healthy before the experiments and might have remained so had the scientists understood how to reverse, or somehow communicate their desired to the gadgets. For instance, "please put the bunny's head back on."

Experimenting on humans was not taboo in the 1940s, and was practiced in many countries as well as in the United States, albeit covertly. Even before testing began on human guinea pigs, some scientists that fiddled with the Aliens gadgets unwittingly were maimed, killed, or something more horrible happened to them. No one will ever know about the "more horrible" since the people simply disappeared, taken by the gadgets to an unknown place, and never found again. At the onset of the program, accidents were recorded "officially," but as the years went by and the program became increasingly shrouded in secrecy, information was shared "unofficially," through the grapevine. It was forbidden to write certain things down; nevertheless, some scientists secretly did so. Information that made it on paper or other storage devices such as tape recorders and photography, was never meant for sharing with other scientists in the program, but was to be forwarded directly to the committee only. Therefore, how many scientists lost their lives from contact with the Alien gadgets no one will ever know.

One of the first injuries recorded took place early in the program. It happened to a metallurgist. He was studying the bizarre behavior of exotic Alien metal while it transfigured during a test. He and a colleague were monitoring a batch of Alien gadgets assigned to them. Scientists doing experiments with Alien gadgets were located in a separate building from where the Alien ship was kept (divide and concur was the theme). By placing some distance between the craft and the Alien objects, the scientists were hoping to eliminate any interference or potential influence that the ship might have on the gadgets. The scientists were concerned that the ship somehow remained in communication with its spawn. Another reason they experimented off the ship was that the ship was a strange place to work. Inside the ship was real life "Alice in Wonderland" stuff. It was nearly impossible to get anything meaningful done while Alien creatures jumped around and harassed the scientists when the scientists were inside the ship.

The metallurgist and a colleague had scattered the Alien gadgets around a large table in his lab. The scientists released a rabbit in the midst of the objects to see if any of the gadgets would activate by the presence of the animal. They observed and waited. They watched for the slightest response from the gadgets as the rabbit moved around the table eating the lettuce. The lettuce was strategically placed around the table so that the rabbit would make maximum contact with all the items that were put out that day. The rabbit did not seem bothered by the Alien gadgets. The rabbit was unaware that any one of them Alien gadgets it brushed up against could snatch it up, skin it alive, gut it, and have it fully cooked in less than a couple of minutes! The job had many hidden dangers, but the scientists ate well.

Knowing the hazards of mishandling the Alien gadgets, it was incomprehensible that scientists working with such volatile objects took the risks that they did. As the rabbit hopped about the table, the scientist noticed that one of the Alien gadgets changed color as the rabbit approached it. Believing that the metal was about to change shape the scientist wanted to hold the Alien object in his hand to get a feel for what was taking place inside the metal. The metal quivered, so he took it to his desk where the light was better. As he studied it under the light of his desk lamp, his face made contact with the gadget. The gadget activated and instantly scooped out the scientist's eyeball! It happened so quickly that the scientist did not have time to drop the Alien gadget, which was still holding his eyeball securely in its scoop-like-claw. His colleague, after seeing what had happened thought that the Alien gadget was attacking his friend and summoned one of the guards posted outside the room in the hall. The guard reluctantly grabbed the instrument with the eye attached to it and slowly removed it from the traumatized scientist's hand. The scientist let go of it as he collapsed to the floor, dazed, as if he had been hit with a baseball bat over the head. No blood spilled from the scientist's eye socket, but he was in severe pain and went into shock. His colleague was perplexed over what to do with the eyeball. He told the guard to remain with the injured man and cautiously took the eyeball along with the Alien gadget, which remained attached to the eye, and put the eye and Alien gadget into the icebox in the lunchroom.

The scientists were unable to save the eye, even though it was not damaged in any way. The doctors that examined the injured man were baffled by the precision in which the eye was removed. No doctors or technique that they were aware of could perform that kind of operation. The Alien instrument, on its own, completed a complex procedure in a split second. The Alien gadget cauterized all the blood vessels without damaging the eye-socket or the eyeball!

Disappearing Act

W hen the scientists began experimenting with the Alien gadgets the gadgets began disappearing. At first, it was thought that a trickster (one of the scientists), was playing pranks on them, perhaps taking the objects from the laboratories and returning them back to the ship. That scenario was impossible because all the labs were equipped with personalized lock systems, and none of the labs had been broken into. The scientists were baffled, but after a few weeks, a pattern emerged. Every item from the ship, regardless of where it was, whether it was in another part of the country, or some other place in the world, vanished exactly three days from when taken out of the ship. The items then emerged back on the ship precisely the moment they vanished, or thereabouts, since time was tricky business on the ship and difficult to gage no one ever really knew. As the scientists had suspected the Alien ship somehow remained in contact with its brood of gadgets, no matter the distance or location from the mother ship.

There was so much magic in that ship that it was practically impossible for the scientists to remain focused on their work. At times, the scientists showed signs associated with psychosis. Their personalities gyrated from giddy to despair and demonic. On several occasions, guards were summoned to the labs to restrain belligerent scientists making preposterous accusations and demands on their fellow associates. One scientist insisted that a coworker kneel down and kiss a ring on his finger, than cried hysterically when his colleague refused the demand. Another scientist threatened to kill a colleague's family if he did not receive a birthday card from him. Two others played like children singing and clapping their hands while talking to make-believe friends.

Those cases are a small sampling of strange happenings that took place and affected many of those involved with the covert projects. Those were not episodes of bored scientists, horsing around with their colleagues, many of those affected had to be restrained and taken off the base. Some of them recovered within a few days or weeks, and had little recollection of what happened to them. In some cases, the scientists were permanently institutionalized.

The scientists were never able to master the Alien gadgets because the gadgets seemed to play mind games with them, kind of a "Simon Says" routine, "do as I say, not as I do." The gadgets did not talk, verbally, anyway, which would not have been surprising, since the Alien gadgets seemed to be able to do everything else, including sending messages to other gadgets and devices, and to the scientists via extra sensory means.

Psychics Try Unlocking the Mysteries

T he committee tried using psychics to unlock some of the secrets of the Alien gadgets. The expectation was that clairvoyants would be less intimidated working in areas that were paranormal in nature than the scientists. From the onset, some of the psychics were unable to cope with what they were shown and put in contact with, and handled some situations much worse than the scientists. Many of the clairvoyants simply "freaked out," as one scientist put it. There were a few who overcame the initial shock and actually communicated with the Alien gadgets, but shortly after doing so more than half of them developed psychosis, and were dropped from the program.

Multiply layers of scientists worked on the highly classified projects. Some knew the truth and the origin of what they were working on. Others were kept in the dark and believed that they were working with advanced (human based) scientific projects for the military and private industry. Communication between the many groups was none existent. All the individual groups reported their findings and results to a single committee.

Each group or unit had two or three specialists chosen from such diverse fields as physics, medicine, engineering, psychiatry, astronomy, parapsychology, mathematics, clergy, philosophy, and several other unnamed disciplines. The committee was comprised of seven individuals. That number changed through the years, as did the numbers of scientists in the program. Some of the committee members came from the ranks of the military, the rest were civilians. The President of the United States personally recruited the members of the committee. That policy changed in the Nineteen Sixties, and the process of choosing members remains illusive.

After reviewing the first reports from the scientists, the committee was certain about one thing, that the Aliens allowed the human race to keep the Alien ship, with its marvels, and terrors, as a gift. Still, some members of the committee were concerned about an extraterrestrial Trojan horse. Committee members were cognizant that the Aliens had the capacity to take back their ship at anytime, why didn't they? The committee members were aware that the Aliens could do that after they learned how independent each individual gadget on the ship was, as was the ship itself. The ship could function without the assistance of the Alien crew. Some on the committee believed that the gadgets were the real Alien crew.

It was apparent to the committee that after the ship repaired itself that there was nothing that could keep it from leaving on its own. The mission of the committee was to find a weakness in the Alien ship. However, the more they probed, the more they realized how weak human technology was in comparison to Alien technology. One scientist exclaimed, "There was no comparison to human and Alien technology, we are merely ova, the Aliens Einstein to the nth degree." That is why every president, beginning with Harry Truman, was unable to confirm the existence of extraterrestrials, but forced to deny their very existence. No president was going to come out and tell the world that Extraterrestrials are on this planet, and in space around the Earth, and can "squash" the human race at will if they so choose!

Two of the psychics brought into the program did what their colleagues could not, and excelled at breaking through a few of the complex barriers put up by the Alien gadgets. The psychics communicated telepathically on a very basic level with the Alien gadgets; like a first-grader directing questions to a college professor. The professors (Alien gadgets) were amused and sometimes made an effort to explain complex material to the first-graders (scientists and psychics). Big discoveries come from many little steps and throughout the years, several little steps fell into place like pieces of a large puzzle.

One of the small steps led the scientists towards a huge breakthrough. The psychics figured out how to unlock the secrets to a certain batch of Alien devices that most of the scientists had given up on. One of those gadgets made openings appear where none existed. That device made it possible to walk through walls or other barriers regardless of the composition or thickness of the barrier. The scientists simply willed themselves through the barrier while in possession of that gadget. The device did not change shape, as did many of the other Alien items when activated. It was about the size of a piece of chalk, the kind that teachers use for writing on blackboards, except that it was black and not white. The gadget had a strange absorption quality to it and gave the person holding it the sensation that he could be absorbed into it as if it were a miniature Black hole. When the chalk-like gadget activated, lights in the area dimmed. The gadget extracted energy from its surroundings. Electrical items in the vicinity such as appliances, televisions, radios, lights, and to some degree, humans and pets, were affected. The device pulled the heat out of the room or area that it activated in. It was as if a cold front had moved through. Scientists using the device often wore suitable clothing (for the sudden chill), which was awkward when temperatures outside were hot and sticky. The person holding the gadget had the sensation of suction similar to holding a vacuum cleaner nozzle to bare skin.

Another interesting device the psychics brought to life served to immobilize a person or animal and kept the victim paralyzed for an indefinite length of time. The device was similar to a laser pointer except for the fact that the beam projected three feet, like a slim version of the Star Wars Light Saber. The Alien Light Saber, instantly paralyzed man or beast the moment the light made contact with the cranium. Under the paralysis, the person or animal remained fully conscious, but unable to move in any way except for the blinking of the eyelids. People touched by the beam from the saber, were literally frozen in their strides and had to be kept from falling (if they were off balance), and let down gently, otherwise they sustained injuries from the fall. They remained in that frozen state as long as the beam made contact with any part of the head. Once the beam was turned off or away from the person, the person regained mobility in a few minutes. Additionally, the person affected by the beam suffered a mild case of amnesia, and disorientation. Those affected never recalled what happened to them moments before, during, and after, the paralysis. One scientist who succumbed to the paralysis during an experiment equated the sensation to a high pitch ringing in the ears and in the mind, accompanied by a mild dizzy spell.

Every breakthrough wetted the appetite of the committee and when the discoveries waned, they became impatiently hungry for more. It was during one such lull that the committee seriously began discussing the use of civilians as guinea pigs. The psychics did not produce the consistent results the committee was looking for. There was too much down time between discoveries, which left large gaps in the workloads of scientists and technicians involved in the various programs. That was unacceptable, due to the vast Alien cargo that begged to be unlocked, and the vast Alien secrets unleashed. One drawback was that placing too much pressure on the psychics quickened their burnout rate (which was high). Qualified replacements were difficult to find and alternative ways and means to extract information remained a constant struggle. Had the psychics made better progress it might have alleviated the committee from making the dreadful decisions they faced. Experimenting on unsuspecting people became a valid option, regardless its distasteful nature.

The decision to experiment on humans posed a dilemma for some of the committee members. How would they carry out experimentation on human subjects and still be able to sleep at night? Moreover, that was only the compassionate component of the problem. There were potential legal issues too, should that evil deed ever get out into the public. Those kinds of questions surfaced more often as the decade of the 1940s, where violations against humans were easier to hide, ended. The era for the "greater good" turned into the 1950s,1960s, and 1970s, where the mood of the nation change radically against Big-Brother type government institutions, to outright mistrust and disdain for higher authority. Americans became more cynical and suspicious of the military and the government in general, as a direct consequence of the Vietnam War, and the President Richard Milhous Nixon saga.

Even the most hard-boiled among the committee members knew that it was only a matter of time before their covert organization faced the real possibly of becoming discovered and exposed. "When that day comes, heads will roll, like at the French revolution with the guillotine," proclaimed one of the scientists in the report. None believed it would happen in their lifetime, but there was always that possibility. Committee members were venomously divided on that one issue. Because of the rift, it was feared that someone on the committee might leak that damning information to the press.

Concerns over using human specimens in the labs were prevalent in the 1970s, but it was also an issue at the onset of the covert program. After reviewing several options concerning the use of people to experiment on in the late 1940s, the first committee resolved their dilemma rather easily. They took the Alien gadgets and performed experiments in the battlefield. The two military personnel that were members of the committee proposed the idea. They made that suggestion to their colleagues on the committee after a briefing with the President and his Chiefs of Staff. At the briefing with the President, they learned that the possibility of America going to war with Korea was highly probable. They learned at the meeting that such a scenario would solve several problems. The committee would set up a MASH unit near the frontlines and receive the worst casualties of the war. Many things remain hidden behind the curtain of battle when the obvious dangers of war go into the equation and overlooked. Few on the committee were excited about the prospects of going into the battlefield and exposing themselves and their scientific people to mortal danger.

Dead soldiers tell no tales. That was the bottom line. Secrecy was paramount and fresh meat plentiful in the hellhole of war. The use of mortally wounded soldiers was no less repugnant back then as it is now, unless they were enemy soldiers. The committee subjected soldiers and other victims of the war to experiments "for the betterment of mankind," and only those with a low probability of survival made the grade.

The Korean War provided the committee with multiple opportunities. They had the use of captured prisoners and enemy casualties to experiment with. They also tested the Alien gadgets for suitability as weapons. However, before the operation got off the ground they had many obstacles to work out. The Alien gadgets mysteriously regrouped back on the ship every three days, so they had to figure out a way to get the ship near the war zone. Moving it created problems. Various unrelated research programs existed that required the ship to remain where it was (the site was not disclosed). Human experimentation was a fraction of the whole program that was taking place around the Alien ship during that time. Cutting off other interested entities was a strategic nightmare and many toes stepped on in the scramble to retain influence over the ship. How, and to what extent the Alien gadgets affected the human anatomy was of the greatest concern to the "powers" in charge. Therefore, control of the ship went to that element of the research group.

Okinawa, Japan, was the place the Alien ship would call home for a time. Okinawa was minutes away by air from Korea, and there was already a large American military presence on the island of Okinawa. At that time, Okinawa belonged to the American military. After the defeat of Japan during World War 2, the Japanese mainland, as well as some of the islands including Okinawa, was undergoing massive economic revamping and infrastructure rebuilding. Okinawa sustained major damage during the war and was a strategic location for American military interests in the area; therefore, it received substantial aid. Due to all the undergoing military construction the installation of a highly classified operation concerning the Alien ship, took place without anyone noticing.

There were already American scientists in Japan that were studying the effects of radiation poisoning on the victims of the atomic war with Japan. Five years earlier in 1945, atomic bombs devastated Nagasaki and Hiroshima. The devastation of that war was still apparent in 1950, when the committee set up its headquarters in the region. The exact location the committee chose for the Alien ship remains unknown. The Alien ship was only located on the island for the duration of the Korean War.

There were those on the committee who had compassion for the Japanese people after witnessing the effects of the bombs on that country. Those committee members hoped to learn enough about the Alien gadgets to undo some of the radiation damage that inflicted thousands of Japanese people. They did not perform experiments on the Japanese. They waited until there was conclusive evidence on what the instruments were capable of before any attempts to treat civilians with the Alien technology proceeded.

In a war situation, where life, death, misery, and brutality, flashed by at a rapid pace daily, few committee members felt that what they were about to do in Korea was wrong. They knew that humanity received a gift, the Alien ship, with its still to be realized unknown possibilities. It fell to the committee to discover and put those gadgets to good use. Others on the committee were more cautious and believed that what they had in their possession could be subverted, made into weapons, which could unleash a nightmare onto the world that would eclipse the horror of the atomic bombs dropped on Japan.

As the committee had expected from the information given to them by sources in their organization, the Soviet-trained forces of North Korea invaded South Korea in the summer of 1950. Within days of that invasion, United Nation troops led by General Douglas Macarthur, entered the fighting and began pushing the North Korean troops back behind the 38th Parallel. Two and a half years earlier the committee had come into possession of the Alien ship. Now, with the war started, they knew they were on the verge of unlocking some of the most fantastic secrets in the universe.

From the start, it was not a smooth running operation. As they set up camp, advancing North Korean troops overran their base. The committee lost doctors and technicians, as well as the Alien instruments. The Alien instruments always returned to the ship undamaged, where they were retrieved repeatedly, not so, for the scientists and technicians who were killed or injured.

Due to the frequent attacks on their base, the experiments were chaotic and often compromised. The stress of being minutes from the frontlines and always in fear of enemy troops overrunning them, took its toll on the staff. Of the three years that the war lasted, only a fraction of the information collected was considered valuable. The bulk of what they had recorded was lost in transit from the moves to avoid enemy fire. Much of what was salvaged was suspect because of the brutal conditions under which it was collected.

The team members chose to work close to the frontlines so that they could work with injured soldiers that were fresh off the battlefield—and with some life remaining in them. The MASH unit did serve in its true capacity and doctored wounded soldiers without experimenting on them. The scientists and doctors only experimented with the soldiers who were beyond hope or enemy.

Nevertheless, some progress happened during those years. The committee was able to forward a breakdown describing the usefulness of certain Alien gadgets in treating disease like malaria, dysentery, and reversing the affects of frostbite and restoring eyesight, by performing complex surgery in the field. According to a report many miraculous recoveries from ailments to war wounds, took place. Unfortunately, many of the methods and techniques performed by the doctors were lost. Those helped by the Alien gadgets included North and South Korean civilian refuges from both sides of the conflict.

That particular committee was not privy to the nature or extent that the Alien gadgets were used as weapons, or even if they were. Any such tests were carried out by other covert units and monitored by other covert committees.

The President of the United States received briefings daily on all findings regarding that project. The President received a summery that described in detail some of the more prominent findings and occurrences from the committee. The report outlined descriptions of the gadgets and some of their capabilities. A sketch of what the gadgets looked like when they "morphed" into operation (activated), and performed their magic was part of the reports. However, the sketches were of little help and only served to show what the gadgets looked like for a brief time during the period it took to sketch them. Change was the only constant concerning the Alien gadgets. Once they activated they oscillated continuously from one shape to another, and sometime their color would do the same. One scientist described the gadgets as having similar attributes as squids and chameleons, with their abilities to change color rapidly, matching their new environment. All of the gadgets in the report were identified with at least one function, although, the report stated that every gadget could possibly perform dozens or even hundreds of other functions.

One report stressed that it would take years of study just to scratch the surface of what these things are capable of doing. For that reason, some on the committee made suggestions to the President, that certain items, those deemed not to pose a national security breach, be released on a limited basis to their civilian counterparts. They were convinced it was time to let the civilian scientific community have accesses to a few of the Alien gadgets. Their thoughts were that something of this magnitude needed study by a broad range of institutions, so that the benefits could be discovered and placed in use immediately.

Others on the committee disagreed and felt that this could be a trap by an unknown race of Aliens attempting to get us to let down our guard, rationalizing that the Aliens might be trying to lure the human race into thinking they are benevolent, or possibly to intimidate mankind by letting humans know what they are up against!

The President received briefings on both views and decided it was bad policy to acknowledge a power infinitely superior to that of humans. The reason, he told the committee members, "was that the sense of balance and security Americans enjoyed could be disrupted by that kind of revelation, possibly damaging the American economy and throwing it, and then the rest of the world, into chaos." He emphasized to the committee that he was not being "melodramatic." The Aliens were far too strange and unknowable and the public not ready to know about that paranormal phenomenon. He then added, "The committee and all of its subordinate units would become more shrouded in their operations, not less."

It was no coincident that expenditures in military projects increased with each succeeding president. The discovery of the Alien ship in 1947 had everything to do with it. The Cold War with the USSR (Soviet Union) was only part of it. Nevertheless, "The Soviet Union was dangerous and unpredictable and deserved keeping on eye on." (A quote in the memo from the president).

After the discovery of the Alien ship in Roswell, many at the top echelon of government were more fearful of things not of this world, than things from this world. Unfortunately, the Soviets, who were already paranoid about the Western world, and looked upon the United States as the only country that could keep them from swallowing Europe whole, mistook the American military build up as a direct threat to them. Therefore, the Cold War escalated to a point that the two Superpowers became the real threat to this planet, more so than any potential Extraterrestrial menace.

Alien Medical Instruments

One discovery during the Korean War was a rectangular device with smooth rounded edges. It was one inch wide by two inches long and had the thickness of one-quarter inch. (Some gadgets such as that one, held their shape longer than most Alien gadgets). The color was sapphire and smooth to the point of slippery, which made it extremely difficult to hold. "It looked like a large precious stone, one that would have rivaled anything found in a prestigious jewelry store," remarked a committee member. However, every gadget in the ship equally charmed those that saw them and worked with the magical gadgets. The Alien gadgets were all seductively beautiful, which belied their immense power to do good and evil.

Placing that gadget on a living body caused it to detected tumors, both malignant and benign. The gadget projected an exact image of the tumor on its screen-like surface. The three-dimensional image rotated and displayed all aspects of the tumor. The gadget only needed to touch the skin once; it then glided a few centimeters over the skin. If no tumors were present, the gadget remained stationary and a cryptic message appeared on its surface. The gadget did not need to scan over the entire body to locate malignancy; it detected problems instantly once the gadget touched the skin. If the cancer had spread, the object moved about the body identifying and cataloging the extent of the illness. The scientists believed that the Alien scanner was mapping the location of each tumor, making notes of pertinent information about the kind of abnormal growth it detected, and then stored that information somewhere. The scientists never discovered how or where the information was stored, whether it accumulated within the object itself or if it transmitted the data back to the Alien craft.

Several gadgets took on the appearance of earthly devices, especially in the surgical category. Often, a surgeon on one of the teams became mortified when an instrument that looked like a scalpel suddenly changed into something else during surgery.

Another gadget on the report from the Korean experiments looked more like a kitchen utensil, a cheese slicer, and not a surgical tool. It had a four-inch-long tubular handle and spatula flat on one end with a slit in the middle of it. The object appeared to be made of the same stuff as the tumor scanner, except that its color was ruby-red. The flat part of the device was about two inches wide and two and half inches long. The thickness was less than a double-edged razorblade. Effortlessly, the device removed skin from one part of the body and miraculously grafted it to another part of the body. No sutures were required to hold the skin in place. Applying the skin to the wound completely healed the wound in a matter of minutes. The device accelerated the healing process at the injury site as it fused the grafted skin to the wound. The condition of the person receiving the skin did not affect the healing process of the grafted area. Lesions and other wounds that did not heal due to underling illness such as cancer or diabetes did not interfere with the healing in the grafted area of the skin.

Skin color did not seem to matter. With that device, they were able to graft skin from one person onto another person with the same rate of success. Skin from Blacks, Caucasians, Asians, and Hispanics, were intermingled with the same astonishing results. The receiving body never rejected the grafted skin regardless where it came from as long as it was from a human. The skin from the donor assumed the color and matrix of that of the recipient at the same rate that it healed.

Mistakes and injuries that occurred early in the program were often due to the expertise of the doctors and scientists, not the lack of it. Scientists tried to assist or force the gadgets to perform in ways they believed the gadgets should perform, sometimes with fatal consequences. Mood and the attitude of the scientists seemed to dictate to what degree the gadgets functioned when they did activate or come to life.

There were markings on some of the instruments, but probably the markings had no more significance than the markings on human based tools and utensils, like trademarks and such. For instance, we do not need written instructions on our knives, forks, screwdrivers, and hammers, to understand their function. The culture we live in teaches us the basics about those things.

One of the most bizarre instruments discovered by the team was a triangular shaped abject about the size of a quarter (US twenty-five-cent piece). Placing the gadget on a person's head, the gadget instantly embedded itself into the skull, rendering the person unconscious. The gadget then lifted the man up headfirst and vanished, taking the man with it. At first, those performing the experiment assumed that the body was transported back to the ship. This was before the advent of "Star Trek," so the scientists were unfamiliar with the famous words, "Beam me up, Scotty." That experiment took place in Korea during the war (to a wounded prisoner). The Alien ship was parked somewhere in Okinawa. They flew to the island where the ship was parked, thinking that the man might be inside the Alien ship with the gadget. They assumed that like the other Alien gadgets connected with the ship that perhaps they had discovered a unique and quick way to get to the ship from any place on the planet. However, the prisoner was not transported back to the ship and was never found, but three days later, the triangular device was back on the ship. The prevailing theory of what might have happened to the man was that the gadget transported him to some other Alien ship in earth's orbit or possibly to the interior of the planet, where clairvoyants suspected that the Aliens had an outpost. A second psychic stated that the gadget transported the body into the sun for reasons he could not understand or explain to the committee. As with all the experiments carried out using the Alien gadgets, that gadget only worked on the living and never on the dead.

Another theory that came from the research team that worked with such devilish devices, was that the soul, or essence of what humans are, had something to do with the destination of the persons carried off by the Alien spawn. Support for that theory came in the course of further experiments with soldiers that lost brain activity during experimentation, due to their war injuries causing the Alien gadgets to cease functioning. The gadgets simply went dormant when the soldier died. Even when the man's body remained alive artificially with life support machines, the lack of brain activity made the gadgets useless. In every situation, the Alien devices/gadgets stopped working the moment the brain waves stopped. It appeared that the Aliens had jurisdiction over humans only to the extent the humans remained alive.

It was painfully obvious to the committee that the Aliens were capable of doing whatever they desired when it came to humans. So what were the Aliens doing with humans? Some questions tossed around by committee members included: How many Aliens and types of Aliens are on this planet? Dozens? Hundreds? Thousands? Did the Aliens want humans to participate by letting humans have access to their ships? Extraterrestrial *Allis in Wonderland* portal ships, filled with supernatural Alien gadgets. For what purpose? Why the secrecy when the Aliens had the means to make themselves known by making formal contact with Earthlings, rather than clandestinely? Did the Aliens stage the shipwreck? Was it a means of introducing their infinitely superior race to our fragile inferior human race? Perhaps the Aliens wanted to let humans know that humans could not survive or handle full disclosure with them? Are the Aliens sowing the seeds for human destruction? If the Government is keeping this little project under tight wraps, are there other projects going on simultaneously? How many covert projects and do other countries have them too? There were plenty of unanswered questions and few definitive answers.

As fragments of the puzzle came together, the committee deduced from the Alien gadgets that the Aliens had an explicit interest in the human anatomy. To what extent, the committee did not have a clue. Since many of the instruments had beneficial features, were the Aliens a kind of behind-the-scene paramedic unit? If so, why are they selective? Thousands of people die every day of accidents and diseases treatable by the Alien gadgets.

At some point the committee switched gears and spent more time brainstorming on the purpose of the Intruders, especially concerning national security. Did the Aliens pose an immediate risk to the country or to the world? That was the main thing for the committee to determine about the Aliens. The committee enlisted the aid of additional clairvoyants and had them concentrate solely on making contact with extraterrestrial beings.

The committee had no access to the Aliens captured when the ship was recovered. During the late 1960s and early 1970s, the committee needed to understand the connection between the abducted and the Aliens. The Aliens had some fantastic stuff, but why did they have that stuff? The committee was denied access to the Aliens that piloted the ship, and were not allowed to know their location or even if they were still alive. To get answers to why the Aliens had what they had the committee needed to find their own Aliens and ask them. The committee used the clairvoyants in various numerical groupings to see if they could concentrate and direct their combined energy to locate Aliens. That experiment failed to produce significant results so the committee was back to square one and they let the psychics work by themselves again. Of the six or seven clairvoyants on the team, one was predicting with 65 percent accuracy on where Alien sightings would occur.

Throughout the decades of the Sixties and Seventies, members of the committee crisscrossed the United States, parts of Europe, and areas in South America, in relentless search for extraterrestrials. The committee never made contact, but they had several sightings. Members of the committee photographed UFOs, chased UFOs with fighter jets and military helicopters, and when the terrain allowed and there were no civilians in the vicinity, they attempted to shoot the UFOs down. They never came close to hitting a UFO, but no one in the committee thought they would. Their intentions were strictly to see if the Aliens would respond, acknowledge them in some way, by blinking their lights or zapping the committee's aircraft with Alien ray-beams, something! "Humor us" was the cry of one frustrated committee member.

After two disappointing decades of seeing UFOs, without making any actual contact, the committee decided to change their approach and focus on "what" or "who" the Aliens were visiting. The committee members read the papers and the tabloids and were aware of Alien abductions. They even interviewed some of the more prominent abductees, but came away with no answers.

The fact that the committee members were part of a secret government agency, with virtually unlimited resources at their disposal, high level contacts, and access to a myriad of public and private institutions, did not seem to matter. The committee ran into the same roadblocks that stymied everyone that attempted to get classified information concerning secret projects.

The committee's existence came about from the Air Force. Those in the know realized the intense competition for special projects between government agencies. There was little chance of favoritism of one branch of government over other branches of government by the Congress of the United States. That held true for the Pentagon. If one department of the military had a secret government committee, then all of them had one, two, or perhaps dozens of secret committees.

The committee did not want to get involved with people that claimed to have been abducted by Aliens (no specific reason was given). The committee was hoping that if there was a department that covered that specific area of research that perhaps the committee could borrow information from that agency. Obviously, someone had possession of the Aliens (dead or alive), and that particular organization had the information that might benefit this committee. Whether it was protocol, government bureaucracy, or basic sibling rivalry, covert committees seldom shared pertinent information with each other. Granted, most were not aware of each other and that was by design. Unable to breach those hidden barriers, the committee performed their own investigations with abductees.

The committee avoided dealing directly with abductees even though the committee knew that some of the abductees were telling the truth. The few abductees interviewed by the committee seemed to have ulterior motives for their claims. Some were interested in a government payout (they would talk all day long about their experiences for a fee) or they were looking to blame their mental problems on Alien or government abductions. Many abductees believed that the government was behind the abduction phenomena and suspicious about talking to people they did not know. That paranoid behavior complicated working with abductees even more. Many of the abductees were looking for their own answers and offered little if any reliable information. The committee needed to know why Aliens subjected those people to abductions, but abductees had no clue why, therefore offered little help.

Detecting a UFO was easier than finding out what the Aliens were doing here. Locating a UFO was only a matter of coordinating their best psychics with the ground and air teams. Once the psychics pinpointed the location where they felt a UFO might show up, the ground team scoured that area until they confirmed the intruder ship. After verification, they dispatched a specially equipped airplane that carried a multitude of radar and other sophisticated tracking devices to that sector. When the Air Force surveillance plane located the Alien ship, they attempted to maintain visual contact with the ship from a distance of several miles, while transmitting pertinent information to the ground crews. The committee never dispatched more than two ordinary civilian vehicles in their attempt to remain incognito during the operation and the surveillance.

The committee members involved understood they were not sneaking up on the Aliens or trying to fool the Aliens in any way; such a ploy against highly advanced Aliens was absurd. The committee was concerned with tipping off ordinary citizens, mostly UFO buffs, who regularly showed up at many of the same places the committee did, regardless the committee's stealthy attempts.

Layers Added to Shield the President

T he committee began reporting all new findings and other discoveries to a newly created agency rather than directly to the President, as they had done in the past. The new procedure went into place between 1974 and 1976 for the sole purpose of isolating the Executive Branch from some of the covert operations.

The committee's first report to the new agency, dated July 30, 1976 (the date itself is a coded message with no significance to an actual day or year). The committee described their failure to identify any persons the Aliens were making contact with on this planet. The duration of the operation was eight months and it produced 271 sightings, but not once had an Alien ship been observed taking or leaving human subjects. Committee members observed Alien ships in residential neighborhoods, in open fields, and in the midst of large cities hovering amid skyscrapers. The duration of individual sightings lasted from a few seconds to one of the longest recorded by the committee that lasted about five hours. The committee concluded that time had no relevance to the UFO sightings. They came to that belief when they noticed that on more than one occasion, when they had visual and radar contact of an Alien ship, people on the street were completely unaware of what took place above their heads in plain view."We were either having mass hallucination among ourselves, and/or the radar and other equipment malfunctioned simultaneously," said one committee member. "We had visual contact as well as equipment contact!" Explained one of the other committee members at the sighting. The logical conclusion was that the Aliens were demonstrating to the committee members at the sightings their supernatural abilities to be seen, or not to be seen, and by whom! It was a disturbing realization to the committee members when they contemplated the implications of what the Aliens were capable of doing.

The whole operation came to a screeching stop because of an emotional breakdown that struck many of the members on the team after that arduous and uncanny investigation. Two committee members had a nervous breakdown; three others developed similar psychosomatic illnesses and were absent for several weeks, two committee members quit the program with no further explanations. It happened the week the committee ended the surveillance campaign. That week was dedicated to hash over and reviewed most of the material from the previous eight months of fieldwork. The details were increasingly disturbing as they tried to ponder what it all meant! They knew they did not have all the facts or possibly none of the facts concerning UFO sightings, but what little they had was distressing and alarming. There are hundreds of mental hospitals in the world that are filled with people who have claimed to see things that no one else (normal people) see. "Are the hospitals filled with the wrong people?" They wondered. "Is it possible that many of the so called mentally disturbed people are actually people that have been abducted and don't know it?" On the other hand, perhaps, the committee members themselves are psychotic and living in a grand illusion that they are in possession of a fantastical Alien ship.

A number of committee members throughout the program have lost touch with reality, or perhaps they came in touch with reality, and therefore were no longer capable of functioning in the chaotic world "normal" people call reality. Nonetheless, some of them ended up locked away, institutionalized, with irreversible psychosis. The number of scientists, committee members, and others that worked around the Alien phenomena that succumbed to insanity remains a dark secret.

At first, the committee believed that contact with something on the Alien ship might have brought on the mental disease. Entering the Alien ship literally altered the minds of those that worked inside the ship. Concepts of time and space faltered while inside the ship. The Alien ship was unquestionably a mind-altering experience. The problem with such theories was that many scientists and others that worked around the same Alien gadgets and spent time inside the ship never succumbed to mental illness. The committee dropped the subject when the higher ups pointed out to them that their job was not to figure out "why psychosis happens but why Aliens happen!"

There was little doubt in any of the committee members' minds that secrecy was the only policy, a consensus agreed to by the new reorganized committee. The thought that there could be thousands of these Alien ships flying around, showing themselves selectively to whomever they choose, was unnerving for those who knew about it. If those in the secret programs could barely maintain focus with that kind of knowledge, much less their sanity, how then would the country or the entire world react if suddenly such information became public? Humanity under a giant microscope and observed by higher intelligent beings was a disturbing reality.

If that information were to get out would people continue in their daily routines of working, buying, playing, investing, and doing the millions of other things that keep the economies of the world churning along? How would the news of Aliens influence the stock markets? Any significant disruption would ripple across world markets and perhaps cause them to fail, destroying worldwide economies. The result would be pandemonium. The planet would be primed for dictatorship. A New World Order would fill the void, possibly a new order installed by Aliens!

Pandora's Box

Although the committee was unable to catch the Aliens in the act of abducting humans, some of the researchers did make substantial discoveries with the items found on the ship. One item discovered inside the Alien ship had the shape of a cigar box. The box performed a similar function as the black chalk gadget. The box created doorways through barriers as did the black chalk gadget, except that the box allowed more than one person at a time to penetrate walls. The box had symbols and three slight impressions on the cover or the lid of the box. The committee members apparently overlooked the box initially, or the Aliens placed the box in the ship decades after the crash. No one could be sure.

The box did not have a lid that swung up or any moving parts to it. The box operated like the opening of the Alien spacecraft, an opening happened, but not by simple desire, concerning the box. The three impressions on the top of the box acted like a combination lock. Entering the correct sequence created an opening on the top of the box and revealed a variety of geometrically diverse objects inside of the box. There was no mention on how the committee broke the code or how long it took them to figure out how the box worked. When the box opened, it automatically engulfed everyone in its vicinity into a strange cloud of electrically charged plasma. A person could walk in and out of the electrified envelope without harm, but it left an eerie feeling with those who experienced it. The envelope resembled an electrified cellophane membrane with defined boundaries, but that was only an illusion. The envelope's capacity seemed endless, there was no apparent fixed range to it; it simply expanded to the people that were there. If two people, the envelope encompassed the two. When there were more people, it embraced the larger group.

The plasma did not reach out to an individual or individuals, or follow anyone that strayed from the main contingent. It sensed protocol and performed accordingly. The envelope allowed those within it to walk through barriers as well as walk on air. Those inside the plasma bubble did not hover; they walked on a solid invisible platform.

Barriers disobeyed the laws of physics when the plasma emanating from the box touched the obstruction. The box was a breakthrough to understanding how the Aliens abducted people from the most bizarre situations: from moving cars, airplanes while in flight, and from skyscrapers through sealed glass windows. The abducted that were interviewed by committee members insisted that doors were never opened; locks were not broken, and that the Aliens simply permeated through walls and into their bedrooms, and carried them or let them walk on invisible platforms to the waiting spaceship.

Among the items in the box, the scientists identified one that subdued humans in a similar way as the laser pointer discovered earlier in the program. That gadget was small and looked like a sewing thimble. The thimble-like object had a green glow that delivered a paralyzing sting to animals and people regardless of their size. During testing, a large bull-elephant touched by the tip of the thimble on its trunk froze instantly and became like a statue. The paralysis lasted about five minutes before wearing off. The gadget produced the same outcome regardless of the size of the animal or human without noticeable or permanent side effects. The Alien thimble needed to come into brief contact with skin on any part of the body to paralyze the subject.

The cigar box contained several odd-shaped objects inside of it. One of the gadgets, a round metallic wafer, no larger than a copper penny, kept a human paralyzed indefinitely when placed on the person's forehead or any part of the head. The wafer attached itself to the head like a magnet on a refrigerator door. The recipient remained motionless until the object was removed. There were dozens of such devices inside the cigar box.

Taking inventory of the gadgets in the eerie Alien cigar box was impossible. The contents inside the box never remained the same (numerically speaking). Sometimes the box was full and other times nearly empty. One theory was that the box existed in multiple places or dimensions at the same time, making the contents available to other unknown entities besides the committee members. The scientists did not describe or talk about the other gadgets in the box other than to say that there were other gadgets.

The one predictable anomaly of nearly every Alien gadget that came out of the ship was that the gadgets returned to the ship every seventy-two hours. Because the scientists removed the gadgets from the ship individually and at different times of the day and night, the items returned in the same sequence. At the very instant that the gadgets returned to the ship, they could be taken out for use and experimentation again. The internal clock inside each gadget reset and began another seventy-two-hour countdown. There did not seem to be a limit on how often gadgets could be borrowed from the ship. However, the Alien cigar box obeyed other rules and was available to the committee for longer periods.

Unlike humans, who pride themselves on keeping some kind of order in their homes, the pots and pans in one designated area or cabinet, the dishes and silverware in another, etc. The Aliens had no such obsession for placement of items and gadgets. Alien objects, gadgets, and things, were seldom found in the same place twice. Instead, gadgets occupied different spaces, nooks, cavities, or voids in the ship each time they returned to the ship. Finding gadgets could be frustrating, or a playful challenge like in child's play, hide-and-seek, all depending on the attitude of the scientists.

Alien gadgets changed appearance on a regular basis. Nevertheless, the scientists that worked with a particular item for a length of time came to understand the gadget's abilities and functions by simply touching the gadget. Often, the people working with certain gadgets became intimate with the gadgets and the longer the relationship the easier it became to recognize unique traits of each gadget.

Changes in configuration of the gadgets were not always subtle. Round gadgets become square, or a combination of shapes and one end of a gadget could be geometrically different from the other end. Gadgets that had the shape of a cube might have the shape of a blowfish the next day or next minute. They even changed shape while in use, which was a dismal sight to witness when the gadget was inside someone's body. A few scientists fainted when they first experienced seeing a gadget mutate inside the body of a person under experimentation. Witnessing an Alien gadget "swim" beneath the skin of humans was a haunting experience. It brought to life the cliché "It makes my skin crawl". As bad as that was to observe, there was nothing more grotesque than watching the Alien spawn morph while inside the person, when that person was awake.

The Alien gadgets that entered the body were less than two inches long and looked like small carrots. Once placed on a living body, the gadget entered through the abdomen. The end that burrowed into the skin elongated itself and then formed a tip like that of a hypodermic needle. Within seconds of placing the gadget thing on the person's body, the thing inserted its tip into the skin, creating an incision the size of a pinprick. After the tip inserted itself under the skin, it sucked the remainder of its liquefied mass through the small incision and into the human's body rapidly.

A comment from one astonished scientist who watched the gadget thing, "At first it was a solid object. It then changed into a worm-like creature and began to enter into the body like a parasite. After the creature's tentacle anchored itself under the skin, the creature became balloon-like. What appeared to be solid instantly turned into a liquid, which was held in place by a thin membrane, like a water balloon. The creature transferred its liquefied contents to the inside of the human body, where it solidified. The creature then moved freely under the skin."

The incision was small, there was no blood from it, and it healed at the same rate that a pinprick to the skin healed. The "Creature" (as it was called from that point on), came out of the body the same way that it entered, but not necessarily from the same location. The time that it spent inside the body varied from one individual to the next. What the creature did while it was inside the test subject's body was not known, but the belief among the committee was that it was used as a transport, carrying things into the body and probably removing things from the body.

It was a blessing that in most instances, the subject who underwent that procedure was unconscious and barely holding onto life, but that was not always the case. There were a few episodes when the subject regained consciousness during an experimental procedure and he was in excruciating pain from the Alien gadget "swimming" freely inside of him. Fortunately, for the scientists, the person associated his pain to his injuries and assumed that the technicians around him were regular doctors and nurses, since they were dressed up in the same green garb that the medical professionals use. In any case, the scientists never let the person remain conscious long enough to realize that an Alien creature was swimming around inside of him.

The Aliens apparently did not believe in anesthesiology, or the scientists had yet to identify the item that performed that specific function. From all the experiments carried out, the scientists discovered that when they anesthetized a person using the standard procedure that was used by doctors around the world everyday, the experiments were compromised. In each case, the Alien gadgets stopped what they were doing and became dormant. The Alien gadgets acted as if the person had died. The scientists concurred that the Alien gadgets must function on the electrical impulses of the body. When the cells are anesthetized, the neurons give off conflicting and inaccurate stimuli, making the task of the Alien gadgets impossible. Apparently, the Alien gadgets use the cells in the body like a network of phone lines by which they navigate the whole body. From that point on, the scientists did what the Aliens probably do during abductions, zap the person with the stun ray and paralyzed them without the use of drugs. Under the Alien paralysis, the person remained conscious some of the time. When he was conscious, he experienced the pain, as well as the terror that came from "not knowing" what was happening to him. The subject could not interfere with the procedure since he was immobilized. In most cases, once the subjects of the experiments were released from the Alien paralysis, they had no recollection of what happened to them, or that anything out of the ordinary took place.

Most of the subjects of experimentation were on their deathbed; therefore, the experimenters felt that those they experimented on had little to lose and plenty to gain. In some instances, the victims had everything to gain. A number of the wounded and injured, whether from a war zone or car accident, recovered from their wounds only because of the Alien gadgets and the experimentations done on them.

From the onset of the covert program, the policy was that anyone working in those capacities and projects that became mortally ill or damaged from an accident that they consent to becoming subjects for experimentation. The thinking of the committee was that no one should do to others what they themselves were unwilling to undergo. After carefully reviewing those stipulations, many objections surfaced. The most prevalent of those objections was outright terror! Committee members would not put themselves into a position where "someday" they might find themselves under the experimenter's knife, with Alien creatures placed inside of them, and paralyzed so that their screams for help fell on deaf ears. The committee eventually amended that clause to only experiment on those who were not aware of the Alien gadgets.

After years of handling the Alien gadgets, the gadgets became increasingly more intimate with their handlers, a kind of "bond" formed between the gadgets and the scientists using them. As bizarre as it sounds, the gadgets shared secrets with tenured scientists that they withheld from new or unfamiliar scientists. All the Alien gadgets performed more than one function, discovering additional traits of the Alien magic came easier to some scientists than to others.

Personality and attitude played a major role in the rate of success a scientist was able to achieve. If his or her demeanor was friendly and they were slow to anger, they tended to be more successful than colleagues with short fuses and hot-tempers. Ironically, those chosen to work in covert programs tended to be from the type "A" personality, aggressive and goal-oriented, unsatisfied if they did not get quick results. The scientists were professionals recruited from the top ranks in their fields of expertise. They were also people with integrity and tended to be beyond reproach. All the members of the committee and the professionals that worked under them went through vigorous screening and they needed to have the highest level of security clearance before they were hired. All of them were believed to be of good character and of good will, with the exclusive objective to serve their country. Nevertheless, those that hired them were mere mortals, with the mortal tendency to fail when it came to knowing the human soul. Alien gadgets had no such flaws, and instinctively understood the heart and mind of a man or woman in the program and allowed itself to be used accordingly. It was believed by the members on the committee that an evil person could not subvert the Alien gadgets, at least not the ones they were toying with. The Alien gadgets could not fall into the wrong hands as plutonium or germs used for warfare could. However, no determination regarding whether the Aliens were benevolent or evil beings surfaced. There was evidence indicating that they could be either one, or both. Most of the gadgets cataloged and identified with performing a particular function seemed beneficial to humans. Other gadgets performed in ways that appeared purely wicked and contradictory to earlier findings.

One item that seemed evil was a 1-inch cube shaped object. It looked like a crystal with a small sphere the size of a pearl suspended in its center. The sphere pulsated with every color in the rainbow. "It was a beautiful thing," was a common utterance of those who saw it. However, its beauty hid its dastardly purpose. Unlike many of the other Alien gadgets, only one function was reported for that gadget. When it was placed on the chest of a person, the sphere left the cube, penetrated the chest cavity, and entered the lung. The sphere would not discharge into anything but a living human lung. It left no puncture wound or any other sign of entry on the body. It was never determined whether the sphere had mass or if it was a ball of photons or some other form of exotic matter or antimatter. Once it completed its task, the sphere reappeared back inside the cube. The whole episode lasted only sixty seconds. Not enough time to study what exactly was taking place inside the lung. After penetrating the lung, the whole body of the victim went into a state of transmutation. The sphere appeared to use the oxygen in the lungs to accelerate its function. Seconds after the injection most of the body vaporized into a whiff of smoke, leaving behind a few body parts such as fingers and toes. The scientists who performed the experiment where not injured even though they were near the body when it dematerialized.

It was a horrifying sight and supposedly performed only a few times. They repeated the experiment to try and document what was taking place in the body after the sphere entered the lung. Spontaneous combustion had been a mystery for many decades and will remain so. The Alien gadget only stirred up more questions about the strange and wicked phenomena. The committee concluded that it was not spontaneous, but had a purpose behind it. That purpose remains a mystery. The crystal cube functioned like most of the other gadgets on the ship, it had a mind of its own and kept most of its secrets from the scientists. How did the sphere in the cube know not to penetrate the lung of one of the scientists that were handling the gadget? It probably would have if it made physical contact with the experimenter. The scientists learned from the mistakes of their colleagues, "never come into direct contact with any Alien gadgets!" Clothing made from most materials and ordinary gloves, seemed sufficient protection from the Alien gadgets. To function, the Alien gadgets needed to come into direct contact with exposed living skin, but not always, some gadgets broke their own rules.

Certain gadgets only operated inside the Alien ship. When those gadgets activated, they triggered a corresponding response on the ship; an opening might occur, revealing hidden rooms or small mysterious spaces. Some of the rooms contained futuristic looking surgical tables and equipment. Others were dark, empty spaces or voids that resonated with mystifying sounds, colors, and vibrations. Few scientists ever entered such rooms, and the few that did were never able to put into words what they found inside them. Some rooms never showed up again after the first encounter with them and other rooms shuffled from one spot to other spots on the ship like in a shell game. Getting lost inside the ship was easy to do.

Some doorways and openings inside the ship remained hidden and unknown. There was no hint to where these hidden spaces, rooms, or compartments, were, except when by accident, or coincidence, a scientist happened to walk by the area where the hidden room was located while in possession of the triggering Alien gadget. Such gadgets seemed internally coded to open certain rooms and freaky spaces. One hidden compartment discovered by accident revealed a small chamber with a single seat inside of it. The seat, molded to support a human form, was in a spot smaller than a broom closet. The seat was made of the same material as the ship, a soft metallic substance, but without cushions. The chamber had a glow to it that was hard to describe, but one scientist said that the glow had a heavy feel to it. The color inside the chamber was yellow, and the air, thick as Jelly.

The chamber was the scariest place discovered on the ship mentioned in the documents. It gave those who saw it the chills. None of the scientists studying the chamber dared sit in the seat. The chamber was not much bigger than a nook in the wall with enough room for the seat and an average size man sitting in it. The scientists tasked to study the chamber submitted a request for a human guinea pig to the committee. They asked for a human guinea pig to test one of their theories. They believed that once a person was placed in the chamber seat the chamber would close around the person, "And only god knows what will happen to that person once the chamber closed around him." How they came up with that theory remains unknown.

The victim placed into the chamber seat was a man in his fifties. He had no living family members or friends. He was a transient hit by a car. The search committee in charge of procuring live human bodies or anything else for the scientists, found him through a network of government hospitals that were set up to provide such services. Hundreds of people end up in sanitariums every year that no one ever shows up to claim. It was from that pool of the forgotten that the committee obtained subjects for experimentation. The man they procured for that experiment had suffered massive injuries from the car accident. He was barely alive when the committee received him. Everything possible to save the man's life was done. When it was determined that he would die, the doctors sutured his wounds, suppressed most of his bleeding, and delivered him to the committee. Two hours after the man's discharge from the hospital, the scientists placed him into the Alien chamber. The man could not sit up by himself and there were no straps to hold him in place. No straps were needed. Once placed on the seat, the seat held him tight as if he were a piece of metal in contact with a magnet.

Seconds after placing the injured man into the clutches of the Alien seat, the gadget that activated the opening of the chamber made an indescribable sound. The sound triggered the chamber to close. Once closed, the gadget-triggering device made other sounds and some kind of process in the chamber began. After a few minutes passed (no one really knows how long he was in there, but it did not seem long), the remote device made more sounds and the chamber opened up like a clam standing on its side. The man inside the chamber stood up and walked out of the clam-like nook. There was no evidence of his wounds and his health appeared perfect. For an instant, the scientists thought they had discovered the cure for all major injuries. However, the euphoria was short-lived. As they watched the man, or what they had hoped would be a mended man, the man walked directly into another room in the craft, a mysteriously hidden room that revealed itself when the living human body approached.

The scientists soon realized they were witnessing a nightmare and not a miracle. The man or "thing", walked past the scientists without acknowledging them. The scientists could tell by the look in the man's eyes that something terrible had taken place. His eyes never wondered, but stared straight ahead as if he were a zombie. The room that the man entered was much larger than the chamber that transformed him. The room was circular and had a bench seat that protruded from the curved walls. After the man entered the room, he sat on the bench and continued to stare with a blank expression towards the center of the room. The scientists tried speaking to the man, but he did not respond, although, his eyes blinked at normal intervals and his breathing was normal. He was operating on autopilot. Whoever was piloting the body before his placement into the nook either bailed out or was kicked out; either way, nobody was home. The scientists gave the body a complete physical and found it in perfect health. It was not until they x-rayed the man that they found something abnormal surrounding his internal organs, the stomach, intestinal track, and his kidneys. The body did not eat or drink nor did it perform the normal bodily functions and remained in top physical health. The scientists surmised that the foreign object in the body was an Alien life support system. The Alien organ kept the body alive, but what purpose could there be for a body with the lights out? The body remained in the room for weeks and then months. It did not age or deteriorate and remained in a dormant state, sitting upright the whole time.

The ship was like the fountain of youth for the scientists also. The scientists working in the ship felt as if their aging process turned off when they were inside the ship. Einstein's theory about time slowing down when matter approached the speed of light did not apply because the ship was stationary, unless the ship took off and the scientists were flying around the solar system without knowing it!

The same week that the scientists discovered the "zombie making machine," as they called it, the committee brainstormed on what purpose the body could have. Ideas ranging from using the body to clean up the lab to putting it to work around nuclear waste sites were not taken seriously by the majority in the committee. They considered doing an autopsy on the body and removing the Alien organ that was sustaining it, but orders from higher-up told them not to tamper with the body. The committee was told to monitor the body to see if the body was being incubated by the ship for a purpose that they could not yet grasp.

What the committee members did grasp, however, was that everything about the Alien ship was self-directed. It seemed that the scientists were only there to observe and allowed to participate on a limited basis. After a few years passed and the body remained the same, the scientists received permission by the committee to perform a few experiments with the body.

Alien Cover-Up

C oncern over the increasing media inquiries and the public's persistence to know more about the "Alien cover up" which snowballed in the late 1970s, forced the military to clamp down and make it virtually impossible for leaks about extraterrestrial craft to happen. Every document and report that was not essential to the committee was destroyed. A new procedure went into place for documents that they kept. The chronological order of everything that happened, every event that took place, had the time sequence scrambled and coded. The committee no longer could keep records and documents for more than a week at a time. It did not matter what they were working on or whether the committee felt it significant to carry a particular project into the next week. At the end of each week, every note, folder, and all documents, were removed from the possession of the committee. The committee could request information it required of past experiments and projects and get access to them with little difficulty, but they could no longer keep their own files as they had in the past.

Security was tighter due to the changing times. Specifically because of the new legislation that went into effect in the decade of the 1970s, *The Freedom of Information Act*, which was adopted in

1966, and amended to allow more information to be accessed in 1974, due in large part to the Nixon Watergate scandal.

Committee members and those under the committee's jurisdiction could not bring anything to work with them. Nor could they leave their assigned areas with anything, not even a pencil. All the things they needed while at work was provided to them. Personnel independent of the committee were the only ones authorized to remove and provide office supplies and other miscellaneous items to the committee and their staff of scientists. The committee could not shred, destroy, or remove anything from the facility they worked in, not even their own trash. Everyone associated with the committee had to pass through a screening room before they entered and exited their assigned work areas. Members had to leave clothing and all personal belongings, wallets, purses, etc., in their locker rooms. They wore special clothing while at work that was collected from them when they left the building. Everyone coming and going from the building had to undergo a body search to make sure no one made notes or sketches of Alien gadgets on them. Anyone inclined to take information out of the facility needed a photographic memory. However, due to the nature of what they were dealing with made such a scenario highly improbable. As one scientist told a colleague, "easier it would be to emerge from a tornado with a hand full of sand than to grasp what was in our labs and still make any sense of that information once we left the building." It was difficult enough to communicate with colleagues about "Alien stuff" let alone someone who had no idea of what they were dealing with.

For those simple reasons, committee members questioned the need for the strong security measures they had to endure. How could they possibly go out and talk about the things they had discovered, when they themselves did not comprehend what they had in their possession. When they went home after work, it was as if they emerged out of a dream-state or a nightmare. Forbidden to discus their work with spouses, other family members, and friends when away from work isolated them even more. They did not speak to anyone about their work, not only for the fear they would be found out (they had no doubt they would be if they talked), but also for the fear that their loved ones would think them insane.

Part of the contract each member agreed to when they signed on for the job was that they would be kept under constant surveillance at work and at home. The surveillance technique was familiar to government personnel, especially those that were adept at working under high security clearances. One system used microwaves as a means of surveillance. The system worked by bouncing microwaves off windowpanes. The microwaves detected minute vibrations on the glass surface caused by talking and other noises. Vibrations are subtle and evade detection by the naked eye. It matters not how many conversations are going on at the same time or other background noise in the room with them. A computer synthesized all the voice vibrations and recreated the conversations.

Stored in the committee's computer memory are the voiceprints of everyone involved with the program. With that information, the surveillance team can zero in on a particular member and listen to his or her conversation whether they are in a car, office building, at home, or out on the town.

In the weekly pep classes given by the committee to department heads, security was the main topic of discussion. At one of the meetings, a security officer with the CIA informed them that prior to President Truman's ordering the dropping of atomic bombs on Japanese cities, fewer than a dozen individuals in the world understood the principles required to build that kind of explosive device. Even now, most people do not understand the physics behind nuclear particles or why manipulating quantum elements produce powerful explosives. Yet, the knowledge to create atomic weapons has spread rapidly like a virus around the world. Many countries now have nuclear capability. The CIA agent told the committee, "It is foolish to think that America is the only country to have an Alien spacecraft in its possession." With that assumption, he told them, it is plausible that the countries with Alien knowledge, regardless of the extent of their extraterrestrial inventory, would use all their resources to acquire more of it.

The fear that Alien information would fall into the hands of the public was secondary. What the bosses over the committee feared most was that a competing country would acquire that information. The public received misinformation since the time the committee came into possession of the Alien ship, for the sole purpose of confusing the public and at the same time making it more difficult for foreign agents to acquire Alien technology. Much of the leaked information originated from an agency that worked closely with the committee and not the committee members.

There was ambiguity about the level of covertness because those who controlled the direction of the committee members had given them specific instructions to withhold everything about the UFO phenomena from the public. Then the superiors contradicted themselves when they gave orders to release certain true information via the underground for the purpose of misinformation. Some of the released material was accurate and truthful, but because of its bizarre nature, it was among the first denounced and rejected by the critics of the UFO phenomena. The campaign to discredit the entire civilian UFO research groups required a small budget. The incredibility of "Beings" from outer space or from other dimensions allowed the campaign to perpetuate on its own and required little effort by the committee.

Power of the Intangibles

Millions of people believe with little doubt the existence of extraterrestrials and certain elements of the paranormal phenomena. Likewise, a large part of humanity does not believe in anything at all, especially when such phenomena defy three-dimensional qualities and concepts such as the five human senses; taste, touch, smell, sight, and sound. Tangible things are what life is about to the vast majority of humans. "Kooks that talk about miracles and the 'Nuts' who see little Green Men with big dark eyes should be locked up. With prevailing public opinions such as those, the committee should not need to take many security measures at all." Comments found in a document. Security measures served to keep information from falling into the hands of foreign agents and competing agencies within the US government. However, foreign governments were the primary targets of the concern. Foreign governments around the world that not only believe in the strange and unexplainable, but also spend huge sums of money and time gathering up as much of that "hokey-poky" stuff as they could get their hands on! Nations and people who are caught up in the "tangible" stuff in life miss out on a whole lot of magic and mystery— the only real stuff in life.

During the 1970s, committee members became hungry in their search for answers. Not necessarily because of increased demands from higher ups, but from a strange and exasperating craving to learn more about extraterrestrials and their reasons for being on Earth. It was a feeling all the committee members held jointly as if they were possessed by a higher unknown power. The committee believed they were on the brink of a major discovery concerning the ship and its cargo. There was no explanation for the sudden obsession with the ship, or what caused it other than there were periods that no one wanted to go home at the end of the workday. They were working themselves to death in the quest for more understanding of the Alien mystery and only wanted more.

In the mean time, vocal UFO groups persuaded a few in the Media to pressure certain congressional representatives to shed light on the UFO Cover-up. The wolf of disclosure was beating at the congressional door. Concern that the door would be kicked open before the committee culled pertinent information from the ship and gadgets kept committee members up at night. The possibility of disclosure and the committee losing control of the treasure they owned seemed real. If the world found out about such projects and other secret projects it would be over for them and perhaps mayhem for the country. However, they had little to fear. Some politicians did pound their fists and vowed to find the underlying cause of such conspiracies, but they only did it for show—to placate that small element of their UFO constituency. The normal average American was uninterested in the UFO nonsense, and most politicians know that. Politicians also understand there is a limit to the fruits of their inquiries into secret government projects and do not expect to receive factual answers concerning UFOs. However, the media did manage to get the Air Force to release some UFO files, albeit insignificant dummy files created specifically for disinformation purposes.

Politicians know, or should know, they are only receiving junk, but they do not care because it makes them look like they are trying to get to the truth. All democracies have limits and the United States with the best version of democracy in the world will never reach the point where the common people have access to what goes on in government backrooms. Nevertheless, there is always a firebrand freshman from the House of Representatives or in the Senate that will come along and attempt to kick the door down, believing they will expose the conspiracy behind unidentified flying objects. After a few weeks or perhaps a few months, like all the rest before them, they emerge with the proverbial tail between their legs, no longer looking for a fight and gladly taking the crumbs of deception thrown to them originally. "There are things in the real world that the general population need not know anything about; extraterrestrials being one of them," a quote from a memo that was sent anonymously to one Senator who tried and failed to get information about the UFO conspiracy.

The committee as a whole was painfully aware that they had secrets and knowledge that they and humanity were not ready to accept and it was a real dilemma for most of them. Many involved with the program, if they had to do it over again, would not. Unfortunately, leaving the program was impossible; they knew too much. Ironically, if allowed to leave with no consequences for doing so, most would not leave. Departure from the program would not remove the knowledge of the Aliens from their minds, and living a normal life with the things they knew was not possible. Their only link to sanity was their ability to be around other people like themselves that were stuck in the same predicament.

Once a connection between the Aliens and the human abductions was made, the committee was sure that it would unlock the secrets of human evolution, and perhaps a few other mysteries about the universe. The committee believed they were close to making that connection several times, but the Aliens managed to elude them. The committee had given up chasing after UFOs, and was anticipating that the Aliens would somehow guide them to their next stage of discovery. They knew the Aliens were watching them, they could feel a mysterious presence. Suspicion arose in the committee that someone in their ranks could be conspiring with the Aliens, or perhaps an Alien in human form was a committee member. After the zombie chamber on the ship restored the damaged human body, the idea that Aliens could take human form was a stark and scary reality. It was possible that the Aliens were steering the committee to that conclusion and that was creepy. The committee suspected that the Aliens could use the body they had in the incubator room as a vehicle to enter into the human realm. "Perhaps the body was a portal for the

Aliens to enter our human world unnoticed!" One of many theories brought up at committee meetings. The body was like a machine on idle; the engine was running, but no one was at the controls. The body sat in the incubator room waiting for something or someone to activate its neural circuits and put it into gear.

People under hypnotic suggestion will do things they have no recollection of doing once they come out of the hypnotic state. That notion was the impetus that got one committee member to suggest that it was possible to make the body "perform" even though it had no conscious mind of its own. That idea opened the door to use ESP (extra sensory perception) as a possible way of controlling the lifeless body they had in the ship. Could the Aliens control the body in that manor? Would the Aliens need to enter into the body or could they simply do it remotely somehow?" If the latter, then perhaps the scientists could control the body with the help of psychics and hypnosis as presumably the Aliens could. Committee members and scientists tossed around such theories to try to unravel the purpose of the body kept alive in the ship. Their first approach to studying that hypothesis was to see if the body would react to psychic thought waves. After several trials, one of the psychics working with the body was able to get the body to move some of its fingers. Unfortunately, that was the extent of his achievements and they gave up on that project after six months of exhaustive testing.

Nevertheless, that experiment produced some negative consequences for the scientists working with the body. A few weeks after they had stopped those specific experiments, two scientists working near the body reported that the body came to life, "as if coming out of a coma," said one report. According to the testimony, "The body got up and danced, and in one instance it turned around and looked right at me and then it screamed a stream of profanity at me." There was another incident where the body attacked one of the scientists who had taken the body out of the ship during a brief period for experimentation. No additional details concerning the attack surfaced.

Those personally affected by the antics of the "body" have refused to enter the Alien ship after those events. One skeptic on the committee attributed what allegedly took place to fatigue by those that made those claims. He told the members that the "so called coming to life" of the body could be explained by the fact that the ship affects people in a variety of psychological ways, altering reality as we humans understand reality. That did not explain the incident that supposedly took place outside the ship, but the committee member reviewing the matter did not believe that incident took place either. Other committee members were convinced that something happened, but they questioned why the body that had not moved for two years suddenly began playing pranks on the scientists. One committee member believed the claims and attributed the phenomena to the psychic experiments done earlier. He postulated that the psychic experiments somehow created an opportunity for poltergeist to enter the vacated brain of the body for mischief. He further explained to the committee, "If psychics are able to have limited success in penetrating and activating the brain of the body, as was shown by the moving fingers, then who was to say a ghost or some other spirit or entity couldn't enter the body also?"

The committee remained divided between those that believed in the possible existence of ghosts and those that thought the idea was ludicrous. It was bizarre that any on the committee could be skeptical of the existence of "strange phenomena" after witnessing all that they had. Nonetheless, there were those in the committee that were not convinced of the existence of poltergeist. More testing took place before the committee members made a final assessment of the paranormal matter. After a few weeks of observing the body in and out of the ship, it became obvious that the body did come under paranormal influence when it was out of the incubator room and off the ship. The scientists concluded that the psychic research had something to do with triggering the ghostly shenanigans as was previously contemplated.

The researchers were able to move the body to any location by simply taking it by the hand and guiding it to where they wanted it to go. When unattended for more than ten minutes at a time the body simply walked back to the incubator room by itself. If the scientists working with the body were not finished with the experiments all they needed to do was take the body by the hand and guide it back to where the experiment was taking place. The body was completely obedient, for the most part.

The committee believed that the eerie yellow glow in the incubator room had something to do with shielding the body from unwanted spirits. After the incidence with the ghosts, they decided to leave the body in the incubator room for several weeks to ward off any lingering entities. They thought that if the poltergeists were indeed attracted by the psychic experiments (in the same way sharks are attracted to blood) then removing the body from the unprotected area (outside of the incubator room), might purge any remnants of transient poltergeists and ultimately solve the problem. Apparently, it worked; there were no more strange behaviors from the body reported. Nevertheless, no one felt at ease working around the body after those freakish episodes. All who had contact with the body were aware that the body was a vehicle that facilitated the entry into this world "Evil and strange things." The body up until that point remained without a name, but after the poltergeist incidents, they named it "Frankenstein."

Biodegradable Alien Gadgets

It was possible that nothing ever left the ship. One person on the committee offered that hypothesis one day as committee members pondered how the Alien ship tracked its cargo. During extensive testing of the gadgets, scientists buried Alien gadgets hundreds of feet underground, and shot some gadgets into space, testing their fortitude to return to the ship. They encased the gadgets in concrete, lead, steel, and a host of other alloys, metals, and plastics. The scientists even sank the Alien gadgets deep into the ocean. No matter what they did with the Alien gadgets, every gadget somehow reappeared back on the ship three days later. Gadgets encased in concrete, metals, and plastics, vanished from the material they were placed into without a trace or hint that they were ever there. It was as if nothing was encased at all. The items did not displace the material covering them; no cavities remained if there were any to begin with. How could it be possible? Of what godly material did the Aliens use to make their gadgets? Gadgets defied scratches, dents, burning and manipulation in any way. Attempts to flatten the gadgets under thousands of pounds of pressure failed. The hydraulic presses were not damaged during the testing, the gadgets simply bounced back as if they were cartoon characters!

Ceramic figurines or models were made of some of the Alien gadgets. The gadgets that continually changed shape and size, a history of their morphing was attempted. The task of creating a genealogy of the gadgets that constantly changed shape was challenging, difficult, and in some cases impossible and pointless. Some gadgets (most) resisted any attempt of photography, or image preservation of any kind. There was no means of infringing on the Alien patent!

Some items never repeated the same shape twice; others cycled through dozens of odd shapes, sizes, and dimensions, and then repeated familiar patterns and traits endlessly.

One quandary about the theory that the gadgets actually never left the ship baffled the committee. If the items never left the ship, where did they go when it appeared that they were removed from the ship? When a gadget was removed from the ship, it was no longer on the ship, a logical and tested conclusion because the gadget seemed to be missing from the inventory on the ship once it was removed. The committee understood there was nothing about the ship or its contents that was logical or predictable. Applying logic to find solutions to the quandaries the committee frequently encountered was their biggest frustration.

Displayed on a panel inside of the ship, located in the area believed to be the control center, there were icons depicting everything that belonged to the Alien ship. The size of each icon was roughly one-half-inch square. The panel that encompassed all of the icons was approximately three feet by three feet. There were over five-thousand icons, but that number changed. When the gadgets morphed so did the icons representing the gadgets. The gadgets and icons were in harmony as if they were one. When the scientists removed gadgets from the ship, the icons representing the gadgets gave off a soft greenish glow.

Some scientists believed that the icons were exact working replicas of the gadgets they depicted. However, there was no way to find out because the icons were inaccessible. Unlike human type control boards, which have access to apparatus by opening panels in the back, front, or side, for servicing and upgrading, there was no means of entry into the Alien instrument panel.

The spaceship resembled a living metallic organism. It had no visible rivets or screws to hold things together, nor were there seams, joints, or overlaps of any kind. The location of the windows and doors were imperceptible from the exterior and confusing from the interior. The ship and its contents seemed to be more organic than synthetic; the ship had no hinges, latches, knobs, rollers, or wheels, only a smooth, even, one-piece skin that encompassed the whole ship.

The ship extracted infinitely more information about the scientists than the scientists could ever hope to collect from the ship. No mechanism was clicking away in the ship to indicate the craft was gathering information on the scientists. However, the ship adapted to some of the awkwardness of the scientists as they fumbled around blindly, attempting to extract some understanding of what they were dealing with. The ship often gave clues on which gadgets activated certain devices and openings on the ship by making the gadget the scientists were working with glow or give off a sound or both.

Whenever scientists were slow at noticing the information that dealt with a specific project they were working on they received subtle hints from the gadgets. There is a correlation on how the gadgets helped scientists solve things and the way we humans solve problems by studying a problem until a solution presented itself. Presumably, the answers come to us from our subconscious mind and we call that inspiration. On the ship, the subconscious mind remains unconscious and so does the conscious mind—little makes sense. The committee theorized that the answers, when they came, came from the ship or from its brood, the gadgets! The subconscious mind, like a navigational computer, works non-stop, to help humans better understand and function in the three-dimensional reality we live in. The Alien ship is a multi-dimensional ship, which contradicts human based physics and concepts. The Alien ship understood the shortcoming of the human inquisitors, and provided them with a few solutions to their queries via baby-steps.

Technology, where does it come from?

T he amount of new technology gathered from that Alien ship and then funneled into practical earthly uses remains unknown. At what rate the technology was dispersed is unknown. Assuming that the documents do not exaggerate how were the scientists able to reverse engineer anything at all from such a complex extraterrestrial ship? Perhaps the answer is not so complicated. Human aircraft are designed on the principles of the aerodynamics of birds and insects. Yet, our best engineers cannot build a bird or an insect. Despite the complexities associated with birds and insects, we are able to extract enough information from them and use that information to build flying craft such as airplanes and helicopters.

How did we integrate Alien technology into our own? As things manufactured in factories, the finished product is the result of many dissimilar processes. The raw materials come from one source and the knowledge of how to process from other sources. It is not necessary to know where one technology ends and another one begins, or for that matter, from where it came; the importance is the result. The technology or bits of information coming from covert committees and labs are mixed in with other bits of information from other sources like universities and corporations. The committee is only one of many sources that are secretly working on "who knows what?" Moreover, who cares? As long as new technology keeps coming and improving how we live our lives here on Earth.

One scientist believed that he cracked the puzzle on how the Alien gadgets vanished and then returned to the ship. He felt that the icons were not only symbols on the control panel, but also the actual gadgets. He proposed that the items carried out of the ship and studied by the scientists were disposable replicas of the icons. If that were true, that would indicate that the lifespan of the replicas, once taken off the ship, was approximately 72 hours. He theorized that after 72 hours, the gadgets dissolved into the atmosphere, leaving no evidence that the Alien gadgets ever existed. That theory fit well with the reports made by people who claimed they been abducted. Abductees reported that Aliens inserted metal objects into various parts of their anatomy, but when asked to produce such objects by the skeptics, they were unable to do so. Up to that point, no one on the committee had proved that the Alien items vaporized, but it was one of their better hunches at that time. It also explained why no one has ever found an Alien artifact, and why there is no evidence that Aliens visited the planet. It answered the big question that UFO skeptics always ask, "If Extraterrestrials are visiting Earth, where is the Alien litter?" One answer to that question was clear to some. The Aliens are not litterbugs. However, not all Alien gadgets followed the 72-hour vanishing rules, and little was disclosed about those Alien gadgets.

The possibility that the icons replicated endless copies of themselves with the same ease as microbiological cells dividing inside of a petri dish was astounding. What kind of world could be possible if we learned to harness a fraction of that magic from the ship and applied it to food and energy production? After a gadget was taken out of the ship and it expired, only then did another one reappear and take its place, which was a drawback for human applications. There was no way or method of knowing if the icons replicated new gadgets every three days automatically, or if only the ones that left the ship were renewed. The scientists were unable to test the theory by marking the items because the Alien material was impervious to human markings of any kind.

The moment "Frankenstein" became part of the ship's inventory an icon of him appeared on the panel with the other icons. If the theory that the icons were the prototypes of all the items on the ship, then perhaps the committee could subject the body to many kinds of experiments and reduce the number of humans needed for experimentation. In order to test that theory, the committee members decided to kill Frankenstein. They could not test that theory on any of the other Alien gadgets because they were indestructible. Frankenstein was flesh and blood, or so they believed. However, after the body was modified by the Alien ship they were not sure. The scientists presumed that the body could be damaged or killed, and they could easily test that hypothesis.

None of the scientists volunteered to kill Frankenstein, even though Frankenstein was in a vegetative state—no brain activity, and presumably not a living entity. Therefore, the committee requested the services of a professional assassin, a hit man, to do the dastardly deed. Mysterious individuals that ruled over the committee and over other hidden government agencies approved the request. The committee was instructed to draft a procedure and timeline on the specifics of the request and then the assignment would be taken care of by the department. The details of the hit were sketchy and not clear, other than Frankenstein was shot in the head at close range using a revolver.

The scientists did an autopsy shortly after Frankenstein was killed. They expected to find and remove the Alien life-support "creature" that wrapped itself around some of the human organs that gave life to Frankenstein. However, the creature or contraption was gone. The autopsy did not find anything mysterious or unusual about the dead body, other than the creature inhabiting it for a few years had vanished. The corpse showed the same amount of decomposing that a normal human cadaver undergoes shortly after death. The study raised additional questions and answered none of the previous questions. It did not prove that the Alien gadgets decay, only that the modified human body with the Alien contraption remained mortal. The icon of the body vanished from the panel on the ship. No eulogy or sorrow from those that worked with the body was mentioned. Instead, most of the scientists were relieved at not having

Frankenstein around anymore. After Frankenstein was gone, a noticeable jump in morale occurred, but those happy days were short. Orders from the top stipulated the desire to produce and add to the ship's inventory additional living corpses.

Alien Contact

One morning, a committee member named Bill, revealed to his colleagues that he had been abducted the previous night! That revelation brought a sense of excitement to the rest of the members in the committee. Bill told his colleagues that the abductions had been going on before he came to the program. Bill then told his colleagues that they too belong to the ranks of abductees. The Aliens allowed Bill to remember that abduction because, as the Aliens put it, "it was time."

The Aliens abducted Bill from his bed during the night. Other humans on the ship with Bill that night were abducted moments before they took Bill. They allowed Bill to "observe" and for the first time in his life not be the subject of whatever procedures the Aliens were there to perform. The other humans with Bill that night were not so lucky, and he had to endure the torment they went through. Bill did not have freedom to move about the ship and was told telepathically were to go and he did. The Aliens had total access and control of Bill's subconscious mind. Under the Alien command, Bill's body moved as if he were a robot. All Bill could do was mentally "sit back" while his body instantly took psychic commands from the Aliens. Bill was not sure which of the Aliens on the craft communicated with him or how many Aliens were on the ship that night.

The Aliens were friendly and constantly assured Bill he did not need to be afraid. When Bill had a question that the Aliens were willing to answer, it was answered quicker than it formed in Bill's mind. When Bill asked questions the Aliens were not interested in answering, they told him so, and then let him know that possibly they would give him an answer to that question sometime in the future.

It was a relief to Bill that the Aliens had him on autopilot, Bill told his colleagues, because his knees were like jelly and he could not keep them from shaking. After working on the Alien project several years, Bill could not believe how unprepared he was to meet the Aliens face-to-face. Bill nearly wet his pants just thinking about his abduction.

Bill knew that what he experienced that night was only the initiation and he was not expected to understand much of the things the Aliens showed him. Bill did remember that there were four adult men in the ship with him. The men were naked and sitting on a bench. They looked as if they were in boot camp, sitting up straight, with forlorn looks on their faces. The men did not look completely paralyzed. Bill watched two of the men turn their heads and look directly at him. Bill recognized the fear he saw in their eyes, it was the same fear he had in his!

Bill told his colleagues that the stars are much brighter when viewed from a vantage point above the earth's atmosphere, and he rambled on about how giddy he felt despite his fear. While the Aliens did their work, the craft was parked somewhere in Earth's orbit. Bill wanted to go to one of the portals for a better look at the stars and to see what Earth looked like from space, but they told him he could not during that visit.

The Aliens were strictly business. Unlike a doctor's office here on Earth, where a patient has time to read several magazines before the visit begins, there was little waiting for the anxious souls that were in the Alien ship that night. One at a time, the men got up and walked into a room that seemed to be as bright as the sun itself. The Aliens emitted no sounds and only the individual that was summoned knew what the Aliens were saying or commanding him to do. After entering the bright room strange gadgets (some similar to the ones Bill experimented with at the lab) materialize all around the man and attached themselves to various parts of the man's body, as if his body was magnetized. Soon after, and seemingly from nowhere, a frail-looking Alien appeared. That Alien, with the help of two other Aliens that had been standing there the whole time, assisted the man onto the table. Everything in the room was polished and orderly. Instruments appeared, did things, and then evaporated out of the area when done with whatever they were doing. The Aliens rarely handled the gadgets, the gadgets appeared completely independent or perhaps the Aliens controlled them telepathically.

The room that the four men walked into that night was similar to the one that was on the ship that Bill and his colleagues often worked in, except that they never witnessed instruments permeate from the walls or appear in flight out of thin air. That was the only room that was familiar to Bill. This ship was much larger, perhaps ten times larger than the Alien ship the committee had in their possession. Bill did not see many Aliens during that abduction, but somehow he knew there were dozens of them on the craft.

Bill watched the Aliens work at speeds that made him dizzy. It was the most frightful thing Bill ever witnessed; all he could think of was getting out of that bizarre Alien ship. It was ironic; Bill waited his whole life for that moment and now that he had it, he did not want to experience it again. Although, after the initial shock of seeing humans manipulated in ways that would have left them paraplegic— had it occurred in the human realm—Bill became less apprehensive about the ordeal.

After digesting Bill's account of his Alien abduction, some committee members wondered if they should be regressed, to explore what kind of experiences they had with the Aliens. None of the committee members knew for sure that the Aliens abducted, them, they only had the word of their colleague, Bill.

Bill advised his colleagues not to go through regression therapy. Bill told them that from what he had seen that night on the ship that he could attest that the procedures the Aliens used on the abducted were extremely painful, and that they were better off not reliving their abduction experiences.

Despite the horror that the Aliens put the four abducted men through, Bill was awed at the level of precision the Aliens and their machines performed. In a bizarre way it was miraculous and comical, he told his colleagues. Had he not been terrified, he might have died laughing at what he saw. The way the Aliens tossed the men around as if they were ragdolls, was perversely amusing. It was like being in a den of "mad" magicians. Strange objects flew and hovered around the room, sometimes stopping over the table where laid the abducted, performed a jig or ritualistic dance, then move about the room swaying and dancing in the air.

Some Aliens looked human, or perhaps they were human like Bill, and were on some kind of internship and observing the madness around them as Bill had. If they were human, they were at a more advanced level than he was because they walked around freely and causally without apparent fear.

Some instruments on the craft appeared to be organic; they moved and looked like large worms and other creepy crawly things. The instruments emerged from what appeared as solid surfaces of the walls, floor, and ceiling inside the Alien craft, leaving no hole after emerging or after retreating back into the ship's surfaces.

Regardless of what was performed on the abducted men, the outcomes were not haphazard." The Aliens literally split one of the men down the middle, cutting him completely in half like a side of beef; seconds later, they put him back together with no blood loss or visible scars. When the Aliens butchered the man, the blood appeared solidified as if frozen. The blood did not flow, spill, or squirt from the wounds and body-parts. One man had his arms and legs cut off with some type of laser beam while conscious! He screamed and yelled in horror, but did not pass out (presumably the Aliens kept him from passing out or going into shock). Bill had the feeling that he was going to vomit, but did not, that too was controlled by the Aliens. The Aliens did not tell Bill that this was a demonstration for him, and possibly for others, but that was the only conclusion he came away with.

For the abducted that night, it was strictly outpatient; there was no lying around convalescing under the care of nurses and orderlies for days or weeks. Once the men emerged from the surgical room, the Aliens returned them to their bedrooms, or to wherever they originally picked them up from. Due to the pain that was endured by the abducted, it may have seemed like they were there for hours, but from what Bill could recall, none of the abducted were under the "knife" for more than two or three minutes. The actual time it took may have been longer or shorter, since the passage of time is difficult to judge while inside the Alien ship.

Civilians Used for Experimentation

There were no problems obtaining injured or sick people for experimentation by the committee. Thousands that have no immediate family or friends fill the rooms of nursing homes and state hospitals across the country and the world. This was the pool of choice for the committee. Nursing homes won out over hospitals as harvesting fields because, as one committee member said, "they are like warehouses of the damned. The lucky ones are barely aware of their surroundings. Many of the elderly are only alive because of the drugs pumped into them daily by the nursing home personnel." The majority in the committee believed that experimenting on such people was more humane than the life they endured while at the nursing homes. "Taking them out of the nursing home was like rescuing them from a fate worse than death. Nothing can be worse than a nursing home," anonymous quote. Even in failing health, and barely conscious, some of the old people perked up when technicians working for the committee arrived to pick them up. At the beginning of "operation gray hair" (not the real code-name) the committee setup a medical team to intercept certain critically ill patients from unnamed nursing homes.

The old and decrepit were a pitiful sight. No one on the committee intended adding to their misery. Only those not cognizant of their surroundings and on the verge of death received consideration for experimentation. It seemed horrible that anyone would do such atrocious things to defenseless people, however, many of the old people miraculously healed from their physical and mental problems with the aid of the Alien gadgets. Most of the old folks suffered from severe forms of dementia, arthritis, diabetes, liver, and kidney problems, and when returned to the nursing home, they were in excellent health. That became a major problem and a dilemma for the committee, which had not anticipated those kinds of results. The committee had expected to be making runs to the city morgue not returning rejuvenated elderly people back to the nursing home. Furthermore, the elderly made a fuss about going back! The super-secret underground committee was not equipped for reestablishing the lives of the miraculously cured elderly, nor did they want to turn the renewed old people loose into society. However, the committee did want to monitor them for a few years in order to gage the progress and verify that the healing was permanent and not temporary. The committee ended up halting the program until they sorted out the complex relocation issues.

Returning people fraught with problems of the aging that were healthier than the nursing home attendants were eventually caught the attention of the media. One such episode nearly blew the lid off the covert operation. The committee moved quickly and severed all links that could lead the events to them. They then implemented a new policy and relocated those who were still in the pipeline to other cities and communities. The committee provided them with new lives and identities.

The elderly themselves never suspected a thing. They assumed that when they became ill paramedics came and took them to a local hospital. They had no reason to think otherwise. There was no mention in the documents on how the committee handled the memory question. Perhaps the committee erased the old memories and implanted new memories into the minds of the rejuvenated old people. The scientists were in possession of Alien equipment that could remove and renew memories. Under that scenario, the nursing home would have been notified that the patient died and was cremated. Extensive background checks were done to make sure there was no family or friends that could complicate matters for those in the program. The media soon lost interest when they failed to find anyone who could give them proof of what happened. A few healthy old people with no story to tell was not enough to keep the media interested.

Myth of Human Autonomy

U nderstanding the Aliens was a slow and difficult process for the committee and scientists. However, that was not the committee's biggest challenge. The committee's big challenge was the arrogance that had developed over the years amongst committee members due to their untouchable status. That kind of ego was difficult to control and it threatened to undue the covert operation. Personality clashes and power struggles between the committee members escalated during the nursing home experiments. The belief that they were invincible blinded some of the members to their primary objective. What happened at the nursing home never stood a real chance of exposing the committee because the committee existed under several layers of bureaucracy. What concerned the superiors was the possibility of the media giants taking a serious interest in what took place at the nursing home and placing more pressure on the American covert system.

With the equipment the committee had in their possession, they had the means to become more secretive than they already were. Only a handful of people in the world know of their existence, but with the use of the Alien equipment, committee members would become "literally" invisible. For a time, the committee members were hesitant of using the arsenal of Alien gadgets they had up their sleeves, especially outside of their comfort zone, inside their protected base of operations. They were afraid that if they bungled a mission and exposed the operation that they, and ultimately the whole organization, could unravel. Those involved with the program, committee members, and the scientists, were under constant surveillance, shadowed by "the clean up team." The job of the clean up team was to dispose of covert operatives along with all their equipment, expeditiously, should a mission become compromised and exposure to the program imminent.

Killing one or all of the covert operatives on the spot was not a last resort, but a certainty, when removing them from the scene expediently was not an option. That probability, small as it was, bothered the committee members the most. How can the scientists and committee members in the field be untouchable and at the same time dispensable? It was a difficult reality for the prima donna committee members and scientists to swallow. Because of the "expendable" clause, the committee limited their exposure and avoided risky assignments that were outside of their protected compound. Fear of being found out was not the only factor that held the committee back, there were other reasons that they delayed taking the Alien equipment off the base and into the homes of unsuspecting civilians. The collective belief in the sanctity of one's home stirred inside the souls of the committee members also. The ability to enter a person's home and go into their bedroom without their knowledge took some getting use to, even for egomaniacs. What made the whole thing acceptable was that the committee was aware that thousands of people are visited (some called it violated) by Aliens every day. A few people know that Aliens abduct them, but the vast majority of humanity has no clue that abductions happen.

We humans place the highest value on privacy; naively believing that our innermost thoughts belong only to us. Such ideas are pure fantasy. Privacy of body and mind is a human delusion. Committee members came to those realizations after being indoctrinated into the secret program and becoming aware of the extent of Alien superiority over humanity. Those working in the program have concluded that one cannot violate a trust of a fellow human being when truth and trust are illusions.

After a few months or years, no one knows how long the harvesting of old people continued, the committee decided that people from nursing homes were still the best and safest place to perform tests and experiments. The old people were docile and ambivalent to the handling, poking, and prodding, done on them by the scientists. However, the scientists went about it differently than they did with their first trials, and abducted their subjects from the care facilities rather than check them out with the help of insiders. The black-ops technicians gained entry into buildings by using the Alien device that allowed them to permeate solid objects and walk through walls. They used an unmarked passenger van to carry them and the equipment needed to the site. The Alien gadgets easily fit into a briefcase and behaved for the most part, which was not always the case with freaky Alien gadgets. The nursing home they picked for their first field assignment was located in a rural area, miles away from a large city. The committee did not have operatives at the nursing home as they once had in earlier programs. This operation was a test to see how well they would perform in uncontrolled environments. The operatives had simple instructions: abduct one patient, and take her for a short fifteen-minute drive and then return her to the exact spot they abducted her from. They hoped to accomplish that mission without anyone at the home knowing that she was missing. They had no plans to do anything to her, other than give her a short hiatus. There were contingencies in place should things have gone awry that were not revealed.

Committee members (operatives) arrived at the destination an hour after nightfall. One of the committee members that drove in a separate unmarked car entered the building first. He entered through the front entrance disguised as a state inspector and told the attending nurse at the front desk that he was there to perform a "surprise" inspection. He was equipped with all the necessary credentials, and if the nurse called any of the health departments for verification, committee members monitoring the calls would intercepted the calls.

While the "inspector" distracted the staff, three of the committee members in the van looked for a dark area near the building that was out of view of the front office. After selecting a spot for their entry they activated the Alien equipment and instantly permeated through the brick wall, or as one of the operatives said, "We were sucked into the building." The three operatives emerged into a room occupied by an elderly woman that looked to be in her nineties. She was sitting alone in a wheelchair in one corner of the two-bedroom unit. There was no one else in the room with her; she appeared to be sleeping. The television was on, but the sound was off. When they passed through the wall, they did not feel a thing; the composition of the wall became as a whiff of smoke. However, the energy field that emanated from the Alien box caused the television and the lights in that room and those in the hall adjacent to the room, to flicker. They had rehearsed entering a similar building back at the base before attempting this exercise, but they did not anticipate having the attendants converge on them all at once, as they did during that live exercise.

There were six attendants on duty that night at the nursing home. When the lights started flickering in that wing of the building all six of them went running to that location. The committee member whose job it was to distract the attendants instead had them so nervous from the surprise inspection that the attendants overreacted. As the attendants converged on the room where the committee members had just entered through the brick wall, the committee members had no choice but to subdue and paralyze the attendants as each of them entered the room. One touch of the Alien wand to the head of the attendants paralyzed them instantly. The committee members then placed penny-sized discs on the temples or the forehead of each attendant, and the attendants remained standing, and fully conscious, but unable to move or talk. The committee had never paralyzed healthy normal people before and never out of a controlled environment. They had six people standing limp inside of that room. The attendants looked like living mannequins with nothing but their eyes moving and filled with fear. Because the committee had not planned to interfere with any of the staff or the operation of the nursing home, they aborted the mission. That training mission determined the difficulty they might encounter when entering a private building with the intention of removing a person without rousing suspicion. In the past, the committee harvested from hospitals and nursing homes, the people they needed with the assistance of insiders. Insiders installed covertly into the management of those institutions by the committee. The new strategy allowed the committee to harvest without any insider connection, the motivation being that they could borrow people from any location at the time of their own choosing. The new system also lessened their exposure by reducing the number of operatives in the field and in the management of private institutions.

Shortly after paralyzing the staff, the committee members removed the discs from the heads of the attendants, freeing them from the paralysis. Although the attendants were wide-awake the whole time, they dropped to the floor as their legs gave away from under them the instant the paralyzing discs were removed. The attendants were disoriented, which was good because the four operatives were in a panic and needed the extra time for damage control. Fifty or more patients were suddenly left unattended, and the fact that anyone could at any moment walk into the building and find all the attendants piled in one of the rooms was a near disaster.

The paralysis wore off a few minutes after the removal of the Alien discs from the heads of the attendants, but each attendant reacted differently. Some took longer to come out of the paralysis, according to the one of the operatives that remained behind to make sure all the attendants revived. He said it took more than five minutes for all the attendants to snap out of their dazed and disoriented condition. The attendants remembered nothing of what happened to them, not why they were all in one location of the building or why they were all laying on the floor. As the attendants one by one regain a sense of normality minutes after the committee members left the building, the first of them to reach a phone called the fire department. The attendants had surmised that carbon monoxide or some other poisonous gas had leaked into the building from one of the furnaces and caused them to pass out. None of the attendants remembered that there was an inspection in progress prior to them passing out. The discs not only paralyzed people, but also left them with some amnesia. The attendants did not remember things that happened to them during and prior to the time that they were paralyzed.

The committee members who were monitoring the phone lines during the operation continued to do so. The operatives listened in on the conversation between the staff member and the fire and police departments. They made sure things were under control before they vacated the area. Only two of the attendants were shaken up to the point that they needed medical assistance and taken to the local hospital for observation. The hospital released them that night; the others had no problems and declined to go to the hospital.

No real damage happened, and the police report indicated that none of the elderly patients sustained injury. The report stated that the staff might have succumbed to the fumes from a cleaning solution found near the area they had their dizzy spells. Shortly after that fiasco, those in charge of the program pulled the plug on the use of nursing homes for good (no one will ever know). They did so for two reasons; first, they knew that all the newly rejuvenated old people would eventually draw attention and possibly give credence to the UFO phenomena. Secondly, the cost of reestablishing the lives of hundreds or thousands of people was prohibitive. The money earmarked for the committee was sufficient for the committee's covert operations; there was no contingency fund for humanitarian services to reestablish rejuvenated humans. If they increased their budget by an additional few million to allow for the added services, they risked becoming visible to the congress, which ultimately funds all government programs, even those they know nothing about.

During the Cold War, it was simpler to finance clandestine operations, but after the collapse of the Soviet Union, funneling money to the committee was a covert and dangerous operation in itself. Increasingly, the funding sources had become the committee's

"Achilles Heel." The committee was told that the funding they received was still appropriated from the National Treasury, but that would not be the source in the future.

Second Encounter

Bill had his second encounter. It happened four months after his first. The Aliens took him while he was working in his office during daylight hours. There were others in the building at the time, but Bill was working alone in his office when it happened. It was around noon that the Aliens abducted Bill. Bill was eating a sandwich that one of his colleagues had picked up for him in the cafeteria down the hall. Bill was eating his lunch while going over a report he needed to turn in that afternoon. An instant later, Bill was in an Alien ship without his sandwich. The Aliens did not give him an explanation why they did not allowed him to finish his lunch before whisking him away. Not that Bill asked, but it was certainly on his mind, and he knew he could keep no secrets from the Aliens. A woman was in the craft with Bill. She was lying on a surgical table, and Bill was standing nearby. She was young, and somehow he knew her exact age; she was nineteen years old. She was naked, yet he felt no sexual desires toward her (despite her attractive features). She was lying on the surgical table with a horrified look on her face. She was terrified and confused with no clue of what was going on. She was not able to talk, but Bill knew all her thoughts, an ESP privilege he did not have during his last abduction. She had her eyes on Bill, and in her mind kept asking, "Why are you doing this to me?" She was not sure if she was being raped or if she had been in some accident and was in the emergency room of a hospital. Bill knew her thoughts, but it was not mutual; she did not know his thoughts. Bill had the urge to speak to her and give her comfort, but he was unable to communicate with her verbally or telepathically. Bill knew she was three months pregnant, but he did not know how he knew those things, or why. As he stood there watching her, her whole life was made known to him. Bill then realized why the Aliens where giving him information gradually, while letting the hundreds of questions that popped into his head go unanswered. No human mind was large enough to hold but a fraction of what there is to know, and only piecemeal at that! The little information that Bill did receive about the woman was overwhelming his mind. Why did he need to know all about her? Bill felt he knew her but did not recall ever meeting her before.

Bill watched as the Aliens removed the fetus from her body and took the fetus to an adjacent room. Another Alien came back moments later and inserted another fetus into the woman. Bill was not told if the fetus was the same fetus they took out of her or if it was a different one. If it was the same fetus, what did the Aliens do to the fetus? The Aliens told Bill it was not yet time for him to know that answer. The Aliens allowed Bill to know that the woman was genetically linked to him. In fact, Bill was her biological father, even though he never met her biological mother. Her mother had been impregnated with Bill's semen on board that same ship nineteen years earlier. That fetus was Bill's grandson! Bill was told that he father many others like her, and it was not important for him to have contact with any of them, nor would it be possible for Bill to have contact with them, even if he was allowed to know who they all were. Bill was not told the identity of the woman, his daughter, other than what they had already let him know about her. She could be from anywhere in the world, they told Bill, and after they returned him to his office he would never see her again.

The Aliens revealed to Bill that the physical body was of little importance. The human body was a mere vessel that held the essence of what humans are. It made no difference that the girl and countless others shared his body's DNA; the identity of a person had no bearing to the physical body other than looks. Bill's genes did not pass on any part of the mind or soul. However, disposition and some traits that a child shares with parents are learned from them as they grow up and are influenced by the parents, and not necessarily a part of the gene pool. The ambiguity of that last statement remained unexplained to Bill, and the Aliens did not feel they needed to clarify it further.

The scope of what the Aliens are doing on Earth would never be revealed to humanity, although, there would be limited information given to some, like the information Bill received. There have been many throughout history given knowledge by the Aliens, mostly in the form of new technology and ideas placed into their heads.

Some of the things that were divulged to Bill by the Aliens seemed pointless, made no sense, and sounded crazy, "Eat bananas on Wednesday," "feed the lions every Friday." Other statements were unclear and confusing as well, "Save the Rain Forest, destroy the trees." Bill felt that many of the answers to his questions (when he received answers) were purposely vague, completely puzzling, plain stupid, and occasionally mean-spirited. Bill believed that the Aliens had attempted to provoke anger in him with some of the answers he received and thought that the Aliens purposely messed with his mind simply for his reactions.

After the Aliens returned Bill to his office, he looked at the clock on the wall and determined he was gone for one hour. Bill had no recollection of the Aliens taking him from his office or returning him to his office. Bill found himself sitting at the desk in the same position he was in before his abduction. Bill's half-eaten sandwich was still there. If it were not for the fact that he was in an area with Alien gadgets strewn around him, he would have chalked it up to having fallen asleep at his desk and dreamt it all. The experience and Bill's memory of it were clear and he pondered what the Aliens told him about his offspring not being his. Bill had two children at home with whom he had a strong bond and felt cheated and overwhelmed at the thought that he sired untold numbers of other children. Bill was depressed after that encounter. No one in his department noticed that he had been missing, which was not unusual since his office door was always closed. Bill took the rest of that day off and told no one in his department what had happened to him. As Bill drove home, he could not help but see a little bit of himself in

everyone he passed. He never felt that his body was "all that special."
Why then did they use him as a human stud?

Envy Stymies the Committee

Two weeks passed before Bill told the committee members about his last abduction. When Bill did tell them they seem disinterested rather than showing excitement as they did the first time he opened up to them. Bill's colleagues were envious and puzzled why no others in the group received the privileges Bill seemed to be enjoying. One colleague accused Bill of making up the abduction stories. They could not understand why the Aliens singled Bill out from the rest of them. Was Bill smarter? Was he better looking? Was Bill's blood type special? The committee members wanted to know why the Aliens could not make themselves known to the whole committee. After all, "they were in this thing together," they reminded Bill.

The committee members had no doubt that Aliens existed, they had an Alien ship filled with wacky Alien spawn, but they had a difficult time believing Bill's abduction stories. They thought Bill became delusional from the many years of working around the freak-show that had become their labs and their lives.

Because of Bill's alleged personal contacts with the Aliens, his envious colleagues accused him of dominating or attempting to dominate committee meetings. During that time, Bill's colleagues voted to have him expelled from the committee. The higher-ups, who believed Bill's link with the Aliens was legitimate, vetoed that request. The higher ups then made matters worse by placing Bill in charge of the committee. Bill's colleagues rebelled, and a mediator tried to patch-up the rift, but it did not work. Lack of cooperation between the members caused the program to be suspended and everyone went home to cool off.

Two months passed before the committee reactivated. Presumably, the department continued operating during that time, probably under the leadership of one of the higher-ups. An operation of that magnitude of importance never shuts down. None of the documents indicated what went on while the committee was absent. Bill remained in charge of the new committee when it reconvened. Some of the original members came back. The obstinate members transferred to other departments. Bill spent the two months vacationing in the Hawaiian Islands. While on the islands, the Aliens visited with Bill daily.

Bill advanced to where he could roam freely aboard the Alien craft. The craft moved at speeds that are inconceivable if taken out of the realm of science fiction, Bill told the committee. The Aliens let him chose the destination, and as it formed in his mind, the craft was halfway to its destination if not at its destination. Bill visited many countries on Earth and even spent time on Earth's moon. Bill also visited other unnamed moons in the solar system. The Aliens declined Bill's request to visit the planet Saturn, a favorite of his since childhood. Bill's father gave Bill a telescope when he was young, Bill spent countless nights watching the night skies, and the rings around Saturn fascinated him. The Aliens told Bill that other parts of the solar system were off limits to him, but that possibly in the future he would be able to visit a few other planets.

It frustrated Bill that the Aliens did not indulge others on the committee. It made it difficult for him to share his excitement with them, since they remained suspicious of him and his tales of adventure. All the committee members did spend time with the Aliens, and presumably been to other planets as he had been, but they were not allowed to remember their adventures. Bill told his colleagues that the Aliens treated them no different from the majority of people that they abduct, except that he was able to verify that it did happen to him and them. Bill's colleagues questioned Bill on why the Aliens abducted them and not let them remember anything, what was the point in that? Bill could not give them answers; he could only relay to them what happened to him, and only what the Aliens allowed him to know happened to him. Many of his experiences remain blocked, Bill told his colleagues.

The Aliens advised Bill to discourage his colleagues from going to anyone for regression therapy. Since the time Bill told his colleagues that the Aliens had abducted them, some of them did not believe Bill and were considering undergoing regression to confirm that it did happen to them. The Aliens pointed out to Bill that they could implant whatever memories they wish into the subconscious mind of humans and that many of the episodes recalled during regression are intentionally painful and misleading. The memories are programmed to dissuade the abducted from learning the truth of what really happened to them during abductions. "A truth that is not for them to know, and is none of their business to know!" The Aliens told Bill that humans in the Western World have the illusion of "personal rights." That belief is not prevalent in the rest of the world because it is not true.

Humans do not own their bodies; they are on loan to them. "To own something," the Aliens told Bill, "means you have complete control of the thing you 'own.' What human has control of his body or anything else for that matter? No human can keep his or her body from dying or from becoming ill. The only thing that humans can do is feed and take care of their bodies, not much more complicated than putting fuel in a car and changing the oil once in awhile. Humans are not even in dominion of their own soul! All the bodies on this planet belong to the Aliens." The Aliens did not disclose to Bill, who owns the soul, just that they, the Aliens, had no claim to that part of humanity.

Gift of Knowledge

O n Bill's last two encounters with the Aliens, they showed him how to perform some of the medical procedures that he and the committee had been struggling over during a few experiments. The new information helped to convince Bill's colleagues that he was a genius, or that he did in fact have contact with the Aliens. Because of the complexity of what the Aliens demonstrated to Bill, Bill could only perform the procedures while inside the Alien ship, the ship in the committee's possession. The ship provided a level of purity that did not exist anywhere outside of it. It was also less strenuous working in the ship, similar to being on the moon with its reduced gravitational pull. Working in the ship allowed committee members to perform with ease and speed that was impossible anywhere else. The purity of the air helped them to think clearer and they performed superhuman feats while in the ship.

Bill showed his colleagues how to repair a severely damaged heart. They operated on a woman badly injured in a one-car accident. She was drunk and ran off the road after leaving a bar. Like the rest of the people that the committee acquired, she had no family and no friends. Doctors at the hospital expected her to die that morning. When the committee received her body, her physician already declared her brain-dead. Her body remained alive, but her heart and liver sustained damaged beyond human ability to repair them. The committee was going to repair her heart and then repair her damaged liver. Bill and two others on the committee were accomplished surgeons prior to coming to the program. Bill was good at his medical profession, but an invisible force, far superior to his earthly training and knowledge guided his hands.

During the open-hearth surgery, Bill left the ship for a moment to get more sutures, or perhaps he left for a bathroom break. They did not have a nurse, so they took turns fetching things. Bill left at a point where the woman's condition was stable. When Bill returned a few minutes later, he found the other two surgeons standing over the dead woman's body. The two surgeons had a confused look on their faces. Outside the ship, they told Bill that everything that they were doing during the operation seemed clear and made sense until he left the ship. They then reverted to knowing only what they had learned in medical school and in their medical practice before coming into the program.

The Aliens gave Bill a gift that he was not aware of until his colleagues mention it to him. Bill had a reservoir of knowledge installed into his subconscious mind that the others did not have. The information came to Bill when he needed it. Others, those who needed to know while assisting him, somehow could access Bill's knowledge. It was obvious to Bill that he was being primed for something larger than himself, but he wasn't sure for what purpose.

Much of what was stored in Bill's head by the Aliens was not available to anyone but him. Bill was not aware of all his capabilities and only became aware when he actually needed the information. Bill was the best doctor in the world and getting better by the day. Bill was able to diagnose and repair afflictions that baffled the best doctors. However, Bill could not publish any of it. The knowledge was not at Bill's disposal to do as he wished. It came when Bill needed it for a work in progress and left as soon as the job finished. Bill attempted many times to write down some of the procedures soon after he performed them, but was unable to make any sense of what he accomplished. Therefore, Bill could not share his knowledge with his colleagues. Which served to intensified the distrust that existed between him and the other members. Some committee members saw that as confirmation that Bill was isolating himself from the rest of the committee.

At some point Bill decided that it was counterproductive for him to work with the others. Bill knew the feeling was mutual. The committee members and some of the scientists had become uncomfortable working around Bill. They witnessed a marked change in Bill and were not sure if Bill was man, machine, or Alien. In their collective eyes, Bill was not human anymore. Bill resigned from the committee and told his superiors he would work on his own projects.

Bill was absent from the office most of the time. When Bill was there, he breached the security system with his unusual mode of coming and going. Bill literally popped in and popped out as if he had mastered the Alien powers of teleportation. The security system that monitored everyone entering and leaving the premises showed that

Bill, who once was the first to arrive at work and the last to leave, was now bypassing the security system and the guards at the gate altogether. This violated the rules that everyone else had to conform too. Protocol prohibited such flagrant entry into covert buildings. In addition, it was impossible for anyone to enter or leave the building without passing through security first. Yet committee members observed Bill working in his office many times, even when the security roster indicated that he was not in the building.

Bill's supervisor approached him with that concern. Assuring Bill that he understood how he was able to breach the security envelop and asked Bill to try and adhere to the same rules imposed on the rest of the department—for the sake of morale. Although Bill was a humbler person than he once was, he felt that his special circumstances allowed him certain privileges. Bill explained to his superior that because of his new abilities the Aliens expected more from him and required more of his time. Bill came and went by way of the Aliens' supernatural means. Bill's new mode of travel allowed him to come and go many times during the day and night, and restricting his movement because of jealous bickering was not acceptable, he told his supervisor. Bill was not beaming up and down from the Alien spaceship as they did on the Star Trek shows and movies. Bill simply appeared, disappeared, and did so only while in his office, "so as not to disrupt anyone's sensitivities or feelings."

Bill's boss recognized the fact that no one could stop him from doing what he needed or wanted to do. Bill was the only genuine connection to the Aliens the committee had to that point, so he conceded to Bill's requirements. Bill had become the committee. No other member made any substantial contribution to the program. At the weekly meetings, the whole focus was on Bill, and what he had discovered, and most important, what he was willing to divulge to the rest of the members.

At one of the committee meetings, Bill suggested that they should not add any more people to the program. "The number of people that were involved with the Alien ship was already excessive," he told the committee. Since it was impossible to shift people into other less secretive programs, Bill suggested that the program shrink through attrition. Even though Bill was exempt from the high security measures, he was against lowering them and had some suggestions on how to make them more secure and less burdensome on the members.

The Aliens gave Bill something that was similar to a computer chip for implementation of the security system upgrade. The chip was the size of a period at the end of a sentence. The chip could be placed anywhere on the body. The chip monitored the location of the recipient twenty-four-hours a day. When placed on the body, the chip embedded itself below the skin and remained visible as a freckle or small blemish. The chip eliminated the need for body searches and allowed the members to come and go with considerably less restraint. The Alien unit that monitored the chip was fashioned to look and perform as a human fabricated machine. The chip contained all applicable information about the individual and allowed that person access only to his or her assigned place of duty. Not surprisingly, everyone seemed pleased with the new security system. The old system was dehumanizing and a humiliating system that included body cavity searches.

How much control Bill had over his superiors at the covert base remained unknown. However, when Bill made suggestion to policy or methods of operations few in the committee or even his superiors challenged him. Those that did, usually yield to his point of view before the committee meeting adjourned. It was obvious to those working around Bill that his insight was much keener, which explained why committee members deferred to his ideas most of the time. Bill's manor became so gentle that it was difficult to get mad at him. Bill never lost his temper, always remained calm and composed. Did Bill have the committee under a spell? Bill himself was under Alien influences. The person that was Bill faded slowly away and something much more than he ever was, or could have become on his own, emerged. In every physical aspect, Bill was the same person. For the committee members and scientists that did not know Bill before his conversion, the slow transformation he went through was hardly noticeable. Bill seemed normal, except for the fact that his IQ and other abilities were off the charts.

Meat Market

The committee added five living human bodies to its inventory. They procured the five mortally injured men from across the country. Details about where the men came from, or from what ailed the men prior to their alteration is unknown. The committee kept the bodies stored in the incubator room until a decision on what to do with them came down from their superiors. The military (army) requested that four bodies be turned over to them upon conversion. Most on the committee were in favor of giving the army all the Frankensteins in their inventory. It was discomforting when the committee had one Frankenstein in their midst. Five Frankensteins in the ship made everyone that worked around those living cadavers extremely uncomfortable. The decision to give up the bodies to the military happened while Bill was away for a few weeks. When Bill discovered what was about to take place, he intervened. Bill was against giving the military possession of the bodies (there was no explanation to why Bill was against it). Bill was the only one on the committee capable of stopping the military from taking the bodies. The military had made plans to acquire the zombie-bodies and nothing was going to delay that transaction. However, once Bill got involved the transaction was delayed indefinitely.

Bill had influenced the high command in other then earthly means. Bill never made it part of the record, but he told one of his trusted friends that he was with the Aliens when they dropped in on a certain army General and abducted him. During the abduction, Bill was not privy to all that was "suggested" to the General by the Aliens. However, the Aliens told Bill that the General would put on hold his request for the living cadavers. There was nothing else done to the General at that time, and the whole episode lasted only a few minutes. The Aliens then returned the General to his bedroom. The General remained unaware of his abduction.

That same week, while on board the Alien craft, Bill found himself in a room with one of the bodies that the committee had recently converted into a Frankenstein. The Aliens told Bill that they were going to take his soul out of his body and place it into Frankenstein's body. The idea of entering a dead man's body terrified Bill. The Aliens assured Bill that it was strictly his choice. If Bill was not ready for that kind of experience, it was fine with them, and they would put it off for another time. Bill decided to do it. The Aliens instructed Bill to enter into an adjacent room. The room glowed with the same color of yellow as did the room he and the committee members called the incubator room. The Aliens wasted no time and quickly placed Bill under a trance. After a few seconds, Bill felt himself become detached from his body and lifted out through the top of his skull. It happened exactly like what Bill had read about in books describing out-of-body experiences. People claiming to have died and then experiencing out of body situation; also know as "near death experiences (NDE)." Such documented cases gave detailed accounts of events that people who had died from accidents or illness and than resuscitated back to life. Some of these people remembered returning to their bodies after visiting with a being of light and sent back due to some unfinished business they still had on Earth. There were hundreds of such reports throughout the world.

As with any paranormal phenomena, there are plenty of skeptics concerning near death experiences. Bill was one of the biggest skeptics of that phenomenon. Bill believed that near-death-experiences were pure nonsense, "that the whole thing could be explained by the chemicals released naturally by a dying body." One of Bills favorite stories (one that was popular in the 1980s) was that when the body was going through the trauma called "death," the person dying simply recalled their birth travelling through the mother's womb. The womb, the birth canal, was the tunnel described by those experiencing near death. According to the skeptics, the bright light of the delivery room is what the dying person sees as he or she desperately tries to keep from sliding into the abyss of death. Some of the stories described how the person who died found himself floating to the top of the hospital room and looking down at his own dead body. Sometimes they observed the doctors and nurses working franticly trying to revive them. Some of the people who died remained on that plane of existence for a short period before returning to their bodies, ending their death experience. Nevertheless, some of those stories intrigued Bill, especially the accounts that involved meeting with other beings after death. Where those who died traveled at high speed in a tunnel that ended where loved-ones, aunts, grandparents, or friends, that had passed away greeted them. The departed often visited with a being that radiated light and pure love towards them. The being of light then revealed to them their entire life without judging them before sending them back to their body to continue with their life on Earth.

Bill did not die, but he did experience the same curiosity of his own body as he hovered above it briefly. Bill knew it was his body, but seeing himself from a new perspective was shocking. He looked different from what he had expected. What horrified Bill the most about the experience was the sensation of the other body, Frankenstein, sucking his soul into it. If it were not for the Alien sedative, Bill's mind would not have been strong enough to survive that transformation, he believed. Once Bill was inside the other body, it felt natural to him. Bill was aware that the body he entered did not need to eat or drink, and that the Alien contraption inside of Frankenstein sustained the body. Bill could not feel the Alien object that was inside the body and was only aware of it because he knew it was there from the X-ray they had taken of the body back in the lab. The body radiated with vitality. Bill was not sure if it was because the body was that of a younger man or because the body was energized by the Alien battery-pack. The body was fully clothed, so Bill did not need to get dressed. Bill took his personal belonging, wallet, and keys, out of the pants of his dormant body and he was ready to go. Before he could ask the Aliens about the picture on his driver's license, they told him to look in his wallet. They took care of; his identity on the license fit his new persona.

The Aliens told Bill to have fun with his new self and take a week to explore how the body felt. To get comfortable using the new body, Bill mingled with people who were strangers, like people at the super market. Bill then set out and went to some of the favorite hangouts where his friends and colleagues might be. When Bill encountered someone he knew, he struck up a conversation with them. Bill was surprised that his colleagues from the committee who were familiar with the body he inhabited had no clue that they were talking to Bill, or that one of the bodies that they feared and worked around in their labs was now having a drink and a conversation with them.

Bill attempted to give himself away by using some of his own mannerisms. When that failed, he tried talking about some of the same likes and dislikes that their mutual friend Bill had. Nothing worked; his colleagues never suspected who he was. They merely assume that they encountered a talkative and friendly stranger, or a spy attempting to extract information from them.

Bill's wife and family did not miss him during that week. It was common for Bill to be away from home for days and weeks. Bill wanted badly to disclose to some of his friends who he was, just to see the expressions on their faces. After giving it some thought, Bill realized the insanity of that idea and the potential repercussion it could have on those exposed to such paranormal reality. Bill walked around the city looking a little closer at the people he passed on the streets and wondered how many of them were counterfeits as he was. There was no way of knowing that answer. The Aliens never gave Bill a clue to that question, but they did tell Bill he would know more about it in the future. Bill thought that if anyone could detect a spark of him it would be his family, so he posed as an insurance salesman and went to his house. Bill's wife refused his solicitations and did not let him inside the house. Bill was glad she refused him entry. It was a "stupid idea," he reminded himself again. If anyone made the connection, it could only prove harmful to their psyche.

That was the lesson the Aliens wanted Bill to learn. They sent him down to mingle with people, knowing that he would want to share his secrets with them. Secrets that he thought were too fantastic to keep locked up inside of him. At times, Bill thought he would go mad harboring such secrets! Bill had a strong need, an unquenchable urge, to tell someone, anyone, what he was capable of doing.

After the week passed, Bill returned to the spot where he was to meet with the Aliens to be returned to this own body. The encounter took place at a house that had a "For Sale" sign on it and was vacant. Bill met with two Aliens disguised as real estate agents, they looked and acted very much human and perhaps they were. In the house, Bill found his real body waiting for him. The Aliens kept Bill's body alive with an external apparatus that covered the mouth and nose. Bill was not comfortable seeing his body with that contraption covering his face. The Aliens sedated Bill and quickly returned Bill to his own body. The Aliens performed a different procedure than what they used in their craft; they used a portable unit that fit into a briefcase. While Bill stood next to his body, the Aliens fitted a device over his head, siphoned him out of the Frankenstein body and deposited Bill back into his old self. It was a different sensation from the first time the Aliens moved him from his body to the Frankenstein body. The procedure was seamless and faster and Bill hardly knew it happened. Bill did not have the out of body experience as he did the first time. After the transfer, Bill needed to lay down for a few minutes to reacquaint with his old, tired, body. The difference was startling.

Days later, Bill returned to the office and convened a meeting with the committee members. Bill told them what he had done and what the implications of that new information meant to them. For those who did not believe him, he described the details of his encounter with them at one of the drinking holes they frequented. Skeptical, his colleagues replied that he could have gotten that information from the individual that he claimed to be. Nevertheless, they admitted that would be insane for Bill to go to those lengths to try to deceive them. Bill told them exactly what they were thinking at the time he met with them, no one could have given him that information. While Bill resided inside Frankenstein, Bill was clairvoyant. Bill knew the thoughts of people simply by visualizing their faces or looking at them. Bill had a feeling that the ESP phenomena was part of being detached from one's own body and not necessarily because he was in a mutated and somewhat paranormal human body.

Talking got Bill nowhere so he offered to let the committee members experience the phenomena themselves. Bill offered to duplicate his experience using one of the bodies that they had in the incubator room and asked for volunteers. Four committee members volunteered to try the out-of-body experience. That surprised Bill. Bill did not expect any one of them to want to try that insane experience, especially because it involved leaving their bodies and entering the Frankenstein bodies. Who in their right mind would want to possess another body as if they were a phantom? Obviously, they were not serious, but Bill called their bluff.

Doing the procedure on others was a first for Bill and he was not sure that he was able to do it. Bill assumed, and hoped, that the knowledge would come to him, as he needed it. As was the case with much of the Alien knowledge, the Aliens gave Bill. Bill explained to the four volunteers that the results of what they were about to experience were not absolute and he could run into unforeseen complications. Once the volunteers realized that Bill was serious, three of them changed their minds and withdrew. Tim, the one member that did not withdraw, was eager to proceed with the out-of-body experiment. Bill took no chances and decided to perform the soul transfer in the incubator room rather than use the portable device left in his care by the Aliens. The portable unit was less complicated to use, the Aliens told Bill when they gave it to him. However, Bill felt comfortable working in the Alien ship. Bill was the only one that preferred to work inside the ship. Most of the other committee members got the willies while working inside the Alien spaceship and avoided it when they could. Bill sensed what the others did not, that Aliens were in the ship at all times, but the Aliens remained invisible. Perhaps the others sensed the same thing, but since they had not yet been formally introduced to the Aliens, they remained uneasy about working in the ship.

The Aliens left the portable system with Bill, and disposed of the body that he had used. They gave him no explanation about why they left the portable unit with him or why they disposed of the body rather than return it to the incubator room.

The Aliens uploaded complicated information directly into Bill's subconscious mind. The Aliens did so because the amount and the type of information they needed Bill to know could never be absorbed by the human mind on its own.

Tim, who had volunteered to do the out-of-body process had second thoughts after he entered the incubator room and faced the four ominous looking Frankensteins. Bill gave Tim time to think about it, but continued to prepare for the procedure, as if he knew that Tim would go through with it. As Bill guessed, Tim's fear abated and he was ready to go. Bill instructed Tim to lie down on the surgical table next to the body that Tim had picked from the four that were available. As the process to remove Tim's soul and place it into the other body started, Bill felt the sensation of time slowing down. Bill thought he was having a panic-attack and feared that he was about to pass out. Bill had the sick feeling that one gets when subjecting a friend or family member to mortal danger, and was powerless to do anything about it. Bill's crisis of confidence occurred when he came to the realization of what he was about to do—remove the soul of a fellow human being and place it into a brain-dead zombie! Many questions raced through Bills mind, what if Tim's soul slipped away during the process. How would Bill capture the freed soul and put it back inside of Tim?" The weight of that responsibility created enormous anxiety inside of Bill's mind. Bill was responsible for initiating something, which only he out of the four men in attendance supposedly understood how to do. Bill had never done such an incredible, mind-blowing, paranormal, soul-manipulating thing like that before it was like playing god!

In the blink of the eye, and to Bill's relief, he saw the same two Aliens that returned him to his body days earlier appear in the incubator room. The Aliens quickly immobilized Bill's colleagues and performed the soul removal procedure on Tim, placing Tim's soul into Frankenstein. The Aliens allowed Bill to watch the whole thing in every detail. The Aliens wanted Bill to learn how to do it right. The event lasted two or three minutes and the two Aliens disappeared as quickly as they appeared. Bill found himself standing in the same spot he was before the Aliens played interference for him. Bill was back to normal, composed, and no signs of the stress he had moments earlier.

Bill's colleagues were not aware that Aliens appeared in the room and assumed it was Bill that they observed. They were astonished that the body-swap took place so effortlessly and congratulated Bill on his amazing god-like abilities. Tim was inside Frankenstein and jumping around the room like a child in a candy store. Tim could not believe that it actually happened!

Tim went over to his old body and glared at it; he then began yelling in disbelief and repeatedly yelled, "IS THAT WHAT I LOOK LIKE!" Tim's excitement overwhelmed him and he passed out. No sooner than his colleagues revived Tim that he again worked himself up and fainted once more. After the second time, they decided to let Tim come out of it on his own, which he did after a few minutes.

While waiting for Tim to snap out of his excitement coma, Bill asked the others in the room if they saw anything out of the ordinary during the soul switch. Moreover, did they feel anything while they huddled around Tim and Frankenstein during the body exchange? None of them saw or felt anything out of the ordinary they told Bill. The three men remembered watching Bill perform with the precision of a machine and were awed with Bill's capabilities. They reiterated to Bill their amazement with the level of expertise he had achieved from working with the Aliens. They expressed admiration for his phenomenal abilities, but they also recognized that his abilities were gifts from the Aliens and not his own. "They had to be," they told Bill. They did not hide the fact that they, as well as others in the committee, were envious of Bill's Alien connections, and they did not appreciate being excluded from direct contact with the Aliens.

Bill told them that he empathized with them, but that it was not his call, or in his power, to give them face-to-face access with the Aliens. Then he revealed what really happened in that room during Tim's out-of-body experience. "He (Bill) was not the one who performed like a machine," he told them. Whatever they had witnessed must have been a mass illusion created in their minds by the Aliens. They argued with Bill and swore that they saw what they saw, and nothing could be clearer, especially in the ship. It then occurred to them that nothing is ever clear in the ship. They told Bill what they saw. They watched Bill working alone on Tim while Alien gadgets buzzed around him, Tim, and Frankenstein, like honeybees at a picnic table in July. Which was unnerving, they added.

Bill told them what actually happened. He was not even at the table when the soul snatching frenzy took place. Neither were any of them! The Aliens had paralyzed the three of them and moved them out of the way, as one moved chairs away from a table in order to sweep under it. In fact, all three of them were put into one corner of the room facing away from the surgical table altogether. The committee members looked like mannequins bunched up against a wall in that room, a frightful sight for Bill, he admitted. The Aliens let Bill watch the soul transfer and he was not placed in the corner with the three of them. The Aliens did not communicate with Bill the whole time they were in the room. The Aliens did the job and then moved the three men back to the spot they occupied around the table and disappeared. Bill figured that the Aliens let him watch so that he would know what really goes on when the going gets tough and complicated.

Tim came out of his shock and told Bill and the others that he was able to read their minds. Tim knew what they were thinking and what they talked about while he was unconscious, but believed he was dreaming. The committee determined after some testing that extrasensory perception improved when the soul became detached from its own body. Apparently, when in a host body, the soul never completely attaches to the host body and remains disconnected enough so that the soul, or the essence of what humans are, remains free to roam the "psychic air waves."

Tim's success, along with the knowledge that the Aliens were keeping on eye on them, gave the other three members the courage to jump out of their skins and test the paranormal waters too. After the other three men converted into Frankensteins, with Bill's help, they discovered that they could all communicate without verbally talking to each other. It was as if they had two-way radios inside their heads. On the down side, there was no way of turning the radios off. That was the drawback; every thought the four men had was available to the other members.

Discipline was necessary before they were able to focus and limit their wandering thoughts to constructive and meaningful dialogue. Distance was not a problem for the mind-wave, neither were barriers like the underground buildings, the places they often frequented. Linked by the mind around the clock required a lot of adjustment and they never fully became comfortable sharing that mysterious space with each other.

Bill had an understanding about the Aliens that his colleagues lacked. Bill did not believe that the Aliens were capable of doing harm to humans, despite the fact that they claimed ownership of all human bodies on the planet. Still, Bill was not sure exactly what the Aliens meant by ownership. Bill's colleagues were concerned about where and how the Aliens acquired the bodies that the Aliens use when they mingle "incognito" amongst the human population. Bill told his colleagues that it was probable that the Aliens grew the bodies that they use in one of their ships orbiting Earth, or perhaps the Aliens did what the committee was doing and harvested humans from the endless pool of people that are dying from illness and accidents everyday.

With the equipment that the Aliens possessed, they could keep humans from death and sickness, why didn't they? Asked several committee members. Bill had no answer other than the obvious one, rapid overpopulation if people stopped dying. The Aliens told Bill that they do not interfere with the soul, but they had equipment that allowed them to remove the soul and place it into another body, as Bill and the committee had learned, but the Aliens also stored human souls in containers on Alien ships and other places on Earth. The Aliens did not disclose to Bill why they place souls into containers other than human containers such as human bodies. Bill was not sure he wanted to know. Bill asked the Aliens about the existence of god, and if the Aliens were god's little helpers? The Aliens did not respond to either question.

Bill received good vibes for the most part from the Aliens that he encountered, but there were Aliens that remained in the background and out of communication with him. Bill was not sure why, but he was thankful that such negative Aliens remained a distance from him. Bill believed that the Aliens in contact with him shielded him from the bad vibrations of certain segments of the extraterrestrials that roamed freely on this planet. Those spooky extraterrestrials managed to get the little hairs on the back of Bill's neck to stand up when they were near him, and he prayed that he never had to meet them face to face.

The Aliens by no means disclosed themselves as angels, nor did they mention that demons walked among them. That facet of the Aliens remained obscured for Bill. It was possible that the Aliens answered that question when they revealed to Bill that their primary concern for humans was the physical part. The Alien ability to move souls in and out of human bodies and other places was merely a necessary function of their work.

Bill was taken aboard the Alien craft shortly after his colleagues briefly experimented with the bodies they had entered into. They let Bill dictate the contents of that meeting. Bill's first question to the Aliens was, "why did they not help people who were dying in hospitals from sickness and accidents that the Aliens could cure? Since they, the Aliens, had the capability to heal illness and repair all kinds of damage that happen to humans.

Their response was, "we take orders from someone higher than ourselves, and just like humans manage to always find someone higher up the ladder to pass the buck to, Aliens too follow orders and are passing the buck." Bill asked them if Aliens are both good and evil. The Aliens replied, "Unlike humans, who make decisions based on what they perceive to be right and wrong, in the realm that the Aliens occupy there is no confusion between the two. In other words, good and evil are tools and exist mostly for a "human" purpose. However, real evil did exist.

Even before Bill had his visit with the Alien, the Alien knew exactly what was going to take place during the visit. The Alien knew what Bill's questions were going to be before Bill had formed them in his mind. What then was the point of the session? Bill asked the Alien. There was no point, the Alien replied, or need for them to have a discussion with humans. The meeting was strictly for the benefit of Bill, to give Bill the opportunity of feeling comfortable working with the Aliens. They wanted to give Bill a sense that he could communicate with them face to face if he wished to do so, the way humans do.

On the ship, located in a separate level from where Bill was visiting with the Alien, was a man abducted earlier that day. Directly after the discussion with the Alien, Bill followed the Alien to the room where the other man was located. The man was lying on a surgical table and prepped for some kind of operation. The man was in his early fifties and in good health, but not for long!

Bill knew what was taking place without anyone saying anything. Bill had watched and was allowed to take part in several similar procedures performed in the past with the Aliens. Most of Bill's internship involved the removal of tumors or fixing other ailments that plagued the bodies of human beings. However, the surgical procedure that was taking place at that moment seemed sinister or evil and contradictory to what Bill had witnessed up to that point.

For that occasion, Bill received a gift, the ability to see into the future, the future of the man who was lying in front of him. Bill could see the man withering away and dying. The man's body infested with cancer and the man racked with pain. Bill saw the man's wife in tears when she learns of her husband's prognosis. Bill viewed the man's three children, two daughters, one sixteen the other eighteen, and a son who was ten. Bill witnessed the agony that the man and his wife would go through as they struggled with how to break the news to their children. Bill was shown the devastation on the faces of the children when they were told about their father's terminal illness.

Bill did not want to see anymore! All Bill could think about was his own family and how they would be devastated under similar circumstances. Bill became angry. He shouted at the Aliens, "How could they do an evil thing as that? Are they angels from Hell?"

The Aliens reminded Bill that it was not their will to do anything bad or good. They simply carried out orders given to them and they were passing the buck. The Aliens could not elaborate more about that incident. They hinted that there was more at stake in that particular family than the dying of a man. Like many things that the Aliens had yet to reveal to Bill, he was not ready to understand the full implication of that one incident. Bill's biggest question was why were they showing all this good and bad stuff to him? Did they expect him to be a liaison between them and humans? How could he possibly fulfill such a role now that he perceived what was being done to humans by extraterrestrials as pure madness? Up until that episode, most of what they revealed to Bill was promising and good.

Bill Asked the Aliens if there were invisible requisition forms stamped on people's foreheads like at a car assembly line to indicate what each human will have done to them in their lifetime? And how do the Aliens determine who gets a tumor and who has one removed? Do Aliens create car accidents or all accidents? Bill had not reached the level where he had that kind of knowledge shared with him. Each new step that the Aliens took Bill through, they allowed him time to adjust. Some lessons required more time than others did. The idea of taking a healthy human and making him or her ill was a tough lesson to comprehend and digest for Bill.

The Journey

Bill was told he would be going to another planet for two months and that he should make arrangements with his family and the committee. Bill's wife was acclimated to the level of security he worked under and accepted his word that he could not disclose where he was going. However, she was perplexed that he would be unable to have communications with her and the children for that length of time. In the past, Bill always found ways to communicate with her regardless of his covert projects.

The committee members, who saw very little of Bill anyway, were indifferent about his sabbatical. Nevertheless, Bill's superiors were excited about him going and asked if the Aliens would let him take a video camera with him. Bill replied that he did not need to ask the Aliens about that, he knew the answer. Bill need not be present with the Aliens for them to give him answers or instructions. All he needed was to have a question on his mind and if the question was urgent, he received the answer instantly.

While Bill was away, the committee members that had made the leap into the strange world of body swapping decided they needed to make a few discoveries on their own (without Bill). In reality, the committee had few other choices. It was either that or disband the operation, since it was obvious to their superiors that they were adding little to the program compared to Bill's contributions. Tim alluded to the fact that perhaps the Aliens ignored him and his fellow committee members because of their hesitation to embrace the paranormal nature of the Aliens. Many in the program lived in terror of the Aliens and their ship, with its hundreds of Alien gadgets that ran amuck inside of it. Their apprehensions interfered with their abilities to understand and make use of what the Aliens put into their hands. Although Tim had the most respect for Bill, he believed that Bill needed some competition from the rest of the committee members. "Why should the rest of the committee be Bill's lackeys?" Tim asked his colleagues.

Tim was certain the committee as a whole would make more progress if they were operating on more than one cylinder. Bill was the only cylinder that was consistently firing—concerning the Alien technology. The rest of the committee was along for the ride. They needed to fire up their own cylinder. Tim had on idea on how to do it.

Tim's plan was that the four of them that had crossed over the paranormal line by entering the bodies while in the incubator room needed to go a little further into that mysterious rabbit-hole. Tim suggested they make a bold move and go on a mission off the base while inhabiting the bodies. As expected, he found little enthusiasm among the other three men for that adventure. The rest of the committee thought it was too risky to enter the bodies without the aid of Bill and the Aliens, and did not like the idea of taking the bodies far from the ship or off the base. Tim reminded his associates that they remained stifled by fear. Tim was willing to take the risk and wanted to know who else was going to move ahead with him. The problem that Tim faced was that most in the committee had become completely dependent on Bill, even though they despised Bill. A few of the committee members believed that the Aliens were not there to monitor their activities when Bill was absent, which was a relief, but also a concern.

Tim disagreed. He had an indescribable feeling that the Aliens were not only watching them during their experiments both on and off the ship, but were there with them in the room during committee meetings even when Bill was not around. Tim believed that the Aliens were silently placing ideas and strategy into the minds of the members. It was during one such meeting that Tim got a strong feeling that he would soon have an encounter with the Aliens.

As Tim suspected, a few days after the premonition he found himself inside an Alien spaceship. The ship was nothing as Bill described it. In fact, it was so fantastic that Tim was convinced he would not be able to describe it to the committee any better than Bill had. The reason that Bill, Tim, or any human is incapable of remembering the inside of an Alien ship is because some Alien ships are in a constant state of flux. The changes taking place inside the ship were subtle and most humans failed to notice the transformations happening in front of their eyes. The environment that Tim was in while in the ship altered continuously, yet he was oblivious to the changes until an Alien pointed them out to him. Tim was on the ship less than one hour, but for him that night was the longest in his life. The Aliens revealed more to Tim on his first conscious abduction than they did to Bill. Tim benefited from what Bill had learned and was able to take in more information because of the mentoring from Bill.

Tim did not see the exterior of the craft, but from what he observed of the interior, the ship was huge. The size of that ship easily surpassed two football fields on the level Tim was on, and there were many levels in the ship above and below him. Unlike some of the shows on television and the movies, Tim did not see Aliens scurrying about the ship, or lounging around inside of an interstellar tavern. Apparently, these Aliens remained in seclusion like monks. Aliens did not seem inclined towards coffee breaks and gossiping about co-workers, or "doing lunch." Alien lifestyle was light years different from how humans interact and carry on daily activities with other humans. The size of the craft indicated to Tim that there had to be hundreds of Aliens onboard the spaceship. Tim asked, but did not get a response for what purpose that ship served. It did not appear that the ship ferried humans around because Tim had not seen any humans. It was possible that just as he was unaware of the changing features of the craft that he was also unaware of all the Aliens and humans on the spaceship.

During Tim's exploration of the ship, he saw on several occasions Aliens in the distance, but once he arrived at the spot where he thought he saw them, as if a mirage, there was no one there.

Tim remembered that the craft had a huge inner court and atrium about eleven stories high. At the top was a clear bubble dome that was like a window to the universe. The glass dome appeared to magnify the size and brilliance of the stars and galaxies. The ship was not in motion, or at least Tim did not think it was. If it was, Tim felt no sensation of movement.

Looking out through the top of the massive structure the view of earth with its single moon was exquisitely spectacular. The only other time Tim felt nearer to heaven was while vacationing in Europe and visiting some of the massive Gothic churches. The ship Tim was in reminded him of those magnificent buildings with their dazzling profusion of arches and columns. The only thing missing was the motifs and paintings from the Renascence masters. Many of the designs in the spaceship were unfamiliar to him, yet very impressive. Judging from the decor the Aliens definitely had a deep appreciation for beauty. The glass of the atrium made it appear that the stars and the planets drifted inside of the ship, or perhaps what he saw were holographic images of stars and planets. Tim was unable to differentiate. It was a wonderfully perplexing experience, he told his envious colleagues.

While marveling at the stars and in a state of bliss, the Alien that had summoned Tim to the ship made his approach. To minimize the shock on Tim the being announced his arrival telepathically before making his appearance. Tim tried to remain relaxed. What helped Tim keep some of his composure was the fact that the Alien revealed to Tim the many previous encounters he had with the extraterrestrials. The Alien triggered something in Tim's mind that unlocked a parallel life he never suspected existed until that moment. Tim discovered that he had known the Aliens since childhood.

Mixed in with mind-expanding experiences, and the joyful reunion of past memories, were horrific and disturbing revelations as well, but Tim did not elaborate on the things that bothered him. Tim fought hard to remain calm as he became more and more aware of his dance through life with these strange Alien creatures. Tim was grateful for the telepathic mode of communication because it kept his voice from breaking and his teeth from chattering. Tim's lack of ability to remain completely calm bugged Tim. He was proud of his fearlessness throughout his life, and few things scared him in life, as did that Alien encounter. Tim, as is true for many humans, falsely believed that control resides within each one of us, but he learned differently that day. That encounter proved to Tim the absolute fantasy of human autonomy.

The Aliens assigned Tim a task. The assignment involved him and the three other committee members that had entered into the Frankenstein bodies with Bill's help. The Aliens instructed Tim to go to a house located in one of the suburbs of a large city not far from the covert base the committee was located. Tim did not reveal the name of the town. For the assignment, Tim and his crew used a van disguised with a phone company logo. Concerning the Alien gadgets Tim was to bring for the mission, the Aliens told Tim that he would intuitively know what to take on the mission when he entered the recovered ship where the gadgets were stored. Tim informed the members that they did not need to worry about using the equipment to transfer themselves out of their bodies and into the Frankenstein ones. The Aliens would do the transfer incognito and monitor Tim's crew while they ventured off the base.

Once again, the committee members excluded from direct extraterrestrial contact were annoyed. They were deep into the Alien phenomena and if Bill and Tim could handle it why not the rest of them? Full disclosure could not be any more horrific than the Frankensteins they had stored in the ship and entered into, or any weirder than the Alien gadgets that occasionally maimed and killed committee members. Two of the military people on the committee had seen Aliens before, but the alleged Aliens were dead and behind thick glass and under the jurisdiction of some other secret government agency.

Tim actually had an answer for his colleagues. Tim told them that the Aliens only showed themselves to humans that had gone through a series of preparations, a process similar to human inoculations, which served to boost immunity from viruses or other Alien contagions. The committee members wishing contact needed to have their "shots" before allowed further awareness and face-to-face Alien contact.

If the series of inoculations are successful, the Aliens place those individuals into a higher category. That category determines if and to what extent a human can participate with the Aliens. There are many programs where humans participate and perform jobs for the Aliens. However, most of those people are not aware of whom they are working for. A small percentage of humans reach the level that Bill and Tim have achieved. The Aliens themselves do not know with certainty, which humans will emerge from the immunization process, and those that do emerge, at what level they will serve in the program, if they are allowed to serve at all. Therefore, who in the committee, if any, would be next to cross that threshold, was anyone's guess. Tim learned from the Aliens that the inoculations, for lack of a better word, were to protect the minds of the humans and to a lesser degree, the physical bodies. The Aliens emit energy that could damage human tissue and impede the human psyche. In some cases, the energy the Aliens radiated triggered psychosis in humans. Other elements of the Aliens and their craft were harmful to humans too, but the Aliens did not disclose what those other elements were to Tim.

Primed For a Mission

The Aliens told Tim that his three colleagues, previously primed for the bodies, were on the craft the same night that he was. During the abductions, the Aliens helped the three men get over their fear of the assignment they were to perform and prepped to carry out with Tim.

Tim and his crew entered the bodies, loaded up the van, and headed to their unknown destination. Tim was the only one with the knowledge of where they were going. They made two stops before they arrived at their destination. Although they did not require food or bathroom breaks, the Aliens told Tim that they could eat and that the bodies functioned normally, after all, they were human bodies. Part of the experiment included mingling in public places so that they would become comfortable with the bodies. After they arrived in the town of their destination, they rented rooms at a motel. The next day they toured the city.

The details of the mission came to Tim during that day. This was a covert operation within a covert operation. The committee members that remained at the base and their superiors had no idea where Tim and the other three members were going, or what they were going to do when they got there. The Aliens made sure that Tim and his crew would not be followed or tracked by those not involved with that assignment. All the committee members, as well as everyone involved in the program, had a chip embedded under their skin. That chip was the main key to keeping track of all personnel in the department. However, the bodies that Tim and the other three men inhabited had no such tracking devices embedded into them. It dawned on Tim that he and his crew were free from the watchful eye of his department for the first time in many years. There was no "clean-up crew" following them around other than the Aliens, and Tim and the other three were free for a few days. If Tim and crew messed up, or were involved in an accident, car or otherwise, the Aliens would remove them from the scene in a split second with the added benefit of not killing them.

Tim took the time to familiarize himself with the streets and alleys that intersected the house that they were to enter later that evening. It was daylight when they located the house. That gave them enough time to make plans on how they would carry out their objective without attracting attention.

Working while inside the borrowed bodies was an incredible experience. The bodies did not require sleep or food and yet remained at optimum energy levels. As the four of them talked telepathically amongst themselves, the one regret they all shared was that they could not keep the bodies they were using. While in the bodies, they felt no pain, no fatigue and had no nagging desires for any earthly stimulants such as sex, drinking or smoking. Even those that smoked did not crave cigarettes while in the borrowed bodies!

Later that evening, even though none of them knew what their mission was, they headed to their assignment. It was 3:00 AM, when their van pulled into the driveway of the target house. The neighborhood was quite, and most people were sleeping. The moon was full, the sky clear, and dogs barked in the adjacent yard. They took care not to make any additional sounds, but did not interfere with the dogs and let them bark. They entered the house through the wall nearest to the driveway. Tim led the way. Somehow, Tim knew which room inside of the house they were supposed to go. Tim went up the stairs, than entered the second bedroom that they came to. Tim instructed two of his cohorts to remain in the hall and watch for any occupants that might wake up and get out of bed. If anyone did leave their bedroom, it was the crew's job to stun the inhabitants with the Alien wand and then put them back to bed. The four of them wore special shoes that were made of a sound absorbing material that muffled creaking floorboards. The men communicated telepathically and made no sounds during the home invasion.

Inside the room was a young boy who had recently celebrated his first birthday. He was sleeping peacefully. Tim's job was to place a small object into the boy's nose and one into his ear. Because it was a painful procedure, Tim had to paralyze the boy first. Tim knew that when he inserted the objects that the boy would wake up and start screaming. While paralyzed, the boy would wake up, but be unable to scream or cry, regardless of the pain. The boy did wake up, but quickly fell back to a sound sleep again. Tim completed the procedure, which took less than two minutes. Because of the boy's young age, they did not need to administer amnesia to him.

Certain humans were prone to develop something akin to an allergic reaction when they encountered Aliens. When the Aliens identify a human with such sensitivity, they enlist the help of humans like Tim and Bill, to provide a buffer, as Tim did with that boy. By using humans to make the first contact, and inserting an Alien antihistamine into the human's body, the Aliens are free to encounter those individuals without causing them harm. The Aliens have employed humans as intermediaries for thousands of years. Most people abducted do not need that procedure, but those requiring it number in the thousands.

Seconds after Tim completed the implants, three Aliens appeared in the room. Tim had a feeling the Aliens might drop in. Nevertheless, it caught him off guard. There was no rehearsal for what took place, no plans or blueprints. Everything seemed to happen spontaneously. It was the best security system in the Galaxy. No one could leak information because there was no information to leak. Tim received instructions telepathically at the very last moment that he required the information. Even though Tim instinctively knew that the Aliens might show up, it was not part of the information given to him. Tim understood that the moment the Aliens arrived his job was completed and that he and his companions needed to leave the area immediately. Tim did not know what took place in the boy's room after the Aliens entered and he and his crew departed. Tim assumed that the Aliens took the boy to their spaceship where the boy experienced his first Alien abduction.

On the way back to the base, Tim told his three companions that the Aliens appeared in the room as he was leaving. He asked them if any of them were aware in anyway that the Aliens showed up. None of them noticed the Alien energy vibrations, nor were they aware of the Aliens showing up at all.

At the base, the discussion centered on their borrowed bodies and how they wished they could keep them. What they had accomplished on their mission did not seem important and was treated as if it never happened. None of them wanted to re-enterer their own bodies, it was like giving up a finely tuned racing machine and going back to the old worn out family station wagon. It took time for them to readjust to their old bodies, the fatigue, the muscle aches, hunger pangs, and they required their coffee breaks back.

During the mission, their vacated bodies remained in the incubator room attached to a system that was similar to cryonics that reduced bodily functions and body temperature.

Tim asked the Aliens what the drawbacks were, should a human remain inside the Alien modified human body for a month or more. The Aliens told Tim that if he or any human remain inside those bodies more than a few days the return to their own body would be distressing. It was not permissible for humans to inhabit a resurrected body for long periods. Neither could humans be fitted with an Alien organ device to boost energy and better health. The reasons were simple; earth would be utopia if such things were available to humans. Creating utopia was not on the Alien's agenda; whether it ever would be in the future was not for them to disclose.

Clones

Tim asked the Aliens about clones and whether the Aliens cloned people? The Aliens told Tim that there are many clones on this planet. Aliens that take human form are not using the empty shells of expired humans; they use human clones. They clone from cells taken from abducted humans like Bill and Tim. Tim told them that he has never run into a copy of himself and was not sure how he would react if he did. The Aliens reassured Tim that since there is over 6 billion people on this planet that his chances of running into a copy of himself were slim.

The Aliens divulged to Tim in what capacities they used clones. They showed Tim how one Alien was able to operate several clones at the same time using mind control. Each clone performed a separate task, or worked in unison like robots, depending on the need. Aliens used clones as laborers for mundane and dangerous work, digging trenches, building functional infrastructure for villages, or working in or around nuclear and other exotic sources of energy that Aliens use for a host of reasons around the solar system.

The Aliens used clones for warfare and as formidable armies, especially in ancient times, but also in modern times. Because the clones look and act like the indigenous humans, the Aliens are able to place them anywhere in the world without anyone taking notice.

The clones are neither robots nor humans, they have no soul and they cannot function on their own. Souls can be inserted into clones, but that is not a common practice. The clones are under the influence and guidance of one or more Aliens who act as shepherds for the clones or as commanders over an army of clones. The clones could function as robots, but it is simpler to use humans with full mental capacity for jobs that require more than a zombie. Humans are brought into the program just as Bill and Tim, because they can function on their own, and if need be, at the discretion of the Aliens.

During a subsequent Alien encounter, Tim learned a little more about the Aliens and was shown some of the other Aliens. The primary Aliens, those on the frontline of human contact, were asexual. Among them are beings that looked as if they fit one sex or the other, but it was not made clear to Tim if they were functioning sexual beings or if genitalia was only window dressing. Some Aliens looked like they were a patchwork of spare parts, real examples of the mythological human Frankenstein. There are short, tall, fat and skinny Aliens; some are pale, gray, black, blue, and metallic in color. Aliens walked, flew, hovered and were capable of peculiar and mind boggling calisthenics. There are humanoids with human facial features and hybrids, human/Alien combinations. Some Aliens looked exactly like humans but they never communicated with Tim, therefore he was not sure if they were human, Alien, or something else.

The Aliens told Tim that they are one of many different types of extraterrestrial species visiting earth. There are layers of other Aliens that are above them and below them in rank, all with their own special tasks to carry out on this planet and throughout the Solar System and the Galaxy.

Back from Utopia

Bill returned from his two-month hiatus and found the committee swamped with material they received from Tim's Alien encounters. The committee was busily interpreting and categorizing Tim's work and had forgotten that Bill was on leave. However, Bill was never out of the loop, as some had believed. Bill remained up to date concerning Tim's evolving status with the Aliens. Bill even had an active part in engineering it while he was away. Bill gave the committee plenty of time to assimilate the new data from Tim before burdening them with his illumination from the past two months. Bill told the committee that he needed to spend time with his family and would return after a vacation with his family. Bill's two children were in college and he spent a weekend with them, then he and his wife took an ocean cruise.

Bill never divulged exactly what he did at work to his wife, and curiously, she never pried into his business affairs. She was a petite, shy woman that kept to herself most of the time, and occasionally volunteered at the local hospital. She and Bill were exact opposites, he was outgoing and loved to mingle at parties, she preferred to stay home and read or do needle work.

However, Bill had changed significantly because of his encounters with the Aliens. Bill was no longer the boisterous extrovert he once was. Bill became pensive and more relaxed about life, and increasingly shunned social events and other public gatherings. Bill also stopped going to many of the "mandatory" committee meetings. At work, when Bill did showed up, he only spoke when he had something he wished to convey to the committee, the rest of the time he sat quietly and pretended to listen to the other members that were speaking. There was no more idle chat from Bill. Bill's colleagues missed that one element about him. Bill was the one with the good jokes and funny stories. Bill's penchant to kid around did not lose him any respect; his friends and colleagues had a deep respect for him. Bill's knowledge and extraordinary ability to grasp and understand complicated concepts astonished everyone that knew him.

Bill was talkative most of his adult life and only changed after his first few contacts with the Aliens. Bill's personality changed drastically after that, and his knowledge seemed to quadruple every day. Bill's colleagues nicknamed him "Spock", after the Star Trek character. Unlike Spock, Bill showed compassion for all people, but he did maintain a strictly business mentality when at work.

Bill's wife told him that while he was away for the two months she did not miss him at all. She was not being sarcastic or vengeful after Bill left her alone for eight weeks. She said she felt his presence the whole time he was gone, as if he had never left. Bill could not tell her that she was with him the whole time. An Alien hybrid had taken on her looks and personality and left in her place.

Because she rarely visited with anyone, it was not a challenging problem.

Bill asked the Aliens if he could take her along with him, the Aliens had conditions, they would not allow her to remember, and Bill could not tell her that they went on a journey together to other planets. Bill agreed, although he would have preferred that the trip be the vacation of a lifetime for the two of them. It was more important that his wife be with him and not at home by herself.

While they were on their earthly vacation, Bill's wife told him about a strange and vivid dream she had while Bill was away. She told Bill that they were at a weird and wonderful place, just the two of them; the kids were not with them. It was like another planet; she knew that because it had more than one sun. The planet had three suns all different sizes. One sun was a little larger than the sun the Earth rotates around; the other two suns were smaller, but each brighter than a full moon. Twelve moons circled the planet they were on and each moon was a different color and size. The moons were all inhabited with people and had enormous cities, magnificent buildings, and awesome natural structures on them. Some of the natural and artificial structures were large enough to be visible from the planet. People could travel without much effort to any of the moons and she and Bill did.

The cities she and Bill visited can only exist in dreams she speculated. "Their beauty surpassed reality." She told Bill. The cities sparkled like diamonds, the streets like emeralds. The food was heavenly and it was the first time she remembered taste and smells from a dream. Like the cities, the food was incredibly delicious, it had to be a dream, food simply cannot be that good, she said. She wished she could share that dream with Bill. It was difficult to describe how wonderful the dream she had made her feel. Had she not known better, she would swear it was real and not a dream!

Bill was surprised how much the Aliens allowed his wife to remember about the trip, the trip that she was not aware she went on. Bill believed that the Aliens were going to mask what had taken place with something that fit more into the earthly mode of dreams. Bill was pleased that the Aliens gave her that gift. It turned out as he wished; they got their fantasy vacation after all!

Nevertheless, they blocked much of what she experienced otherwise her ability to live a normal life on this planet would have been compromised. Some of the activities were so fantastically stimulating that both Bill and his wife needed sedation to keep their senses from exploding. They had to wear special bodies that were suited to the alien environment. Bill's body and his wife's body remained on a ship back in Earth's solar system while they traveled to the stars. Night and day occurred on certain moons but was nothing like on earth. The planet they visited had mostly sunny days due to the three stars. Each moon was a unique wonderland of adventure. One moon was a botanical marvel with millions of acres of lush rainforest that harbored numerous species of orchids and various exotic plants and flowers. Some moons were fantasy theme parks where visitors explored their fantasies. Other moons were winter wonderlands with enormous ski slopes and numerous other wintertime activities, which boggled the human mind. There were zoological parks with hundreds of exotic animal groups in natural habitats. Many of the animals Bill had never seen before. Water worlds, or more appropriately, water moons, with endless miles of pristine sandy beaches. Water sports including deep-sea exploration that would make a Jacques Cousteau green with envy, made Bill and his wife wish they could stay there forever. Endless entertainment was available to all members of that planet, the moons, and the tourists, from other planets in that solar system, including from other solar systems, as was the case with Bill and his wife. The moons were not the same size, but some of them were as large as the earth. The planet itself was enormous, bigger than Jupiter.

Bill was forbidden to reveal these experiences to anyone other than the committee. The Aliens were not afraid that Bill would leak out damaging information about them to the public, or to his wife. They were concerned that Bill would look foolish to his wife and his friends if he revealed even a small portion of what he experienced. Bill had the discipline to keep himself from telling the public, but it required extraordinary discipline to keep certain secrets from family and friends.

The most difficult time for Bill came when the Aliens abducted his daughter and she woke up with her nose bleeding one morning. Bill knew what happened to her and what the Aliens put her through, but he had to make up a story about what might have caused her nosebleed. When Bill was young, his parents told him it was something that happened to most children, and that is what he told his daughter too.

Bill's daughter was twelve when he came to know the Aliens personally. Bill was present at one of her abductions and asked not to be invited to anymore of them. It was difficult enough for him to watch someone else's child crying during some of the procedures and be unable to comfort them. It was completely unbearable to watch his own child undergoing such experiences, especially when the child looked up at him and begged him to help her. All Bill could do was observe and agonize. Bill understood some of the things that took place and why the Aliens did what they did. The things Bill did not understand were the most painful. If Bill woke up one day and discovered that the Aliens were doing evil things to him and his family, it would not matter. There is no way Bill could turn the Aliens off. The United States military and all the militaries of the world combined cannot stop or hinder the Aliens in anyway.

Bill was glad that down deep inside he believed the Aliens to be altruistic and worked willingly with the Aliens. However, Bill did have a twinge of suspicion in the back of his mind about the Aliens. Bill never felt that he was a slave to the Aliens, but because they were able to implant any reality into his mind, he was never completely sure of their true intentions.

The Aliens understood Bill's suspicions and told Bill that his ability to be suspicious of them was proof that they lacked absolute control over his mind, otherwise they could easily mask over any doubts in his mind. Because the Aliens have the upper hand in human affairs, they are able to work with humans without glossing over every feeling of mistrust humans will conjure up.

Bill met others like himself during his two months off planet Earth. Not all of the others were from Earth. Those not of Earth shared similar characteristics as humans because they shared similar DNA. Bill met with seven that were from other planets. The seven represented two planets that were exact duplicates of planet Earth. Millions of planets are similar to Earth in the Milky Way galaxy and billions of planets are significantly different from Earth. The planets that were different from Earth had no relevance for Bill and the others and therefore not discussed by the Aliens.

One of the highlights for Bill and the others in his group happened when an Alien triggered a universal language in them. It was the first demonstration the Aliens did for them and it took place while Bill was with the first group. The conference took place in a magnificent courtyard somewhere in the main city. The Alien spoke a single word to those present. That word acted as an access code that triggered something inside the brains of Bill and those with him. Once the Alien spoke the word, a small area of the brain previously dormant in all those in the room, activated, and they were able to communicate with the same language. The bodies each one of them occupied where similar to their own bodies that were left behind.

Bill was surprises to discover that there were twelve others like him from planet earth. The twelve were in the second group that his first group eventually merged with. Bill and the committee members had theorized earlier in the program that there had to be other countries on earth with Alien spacecraft and technology, but had no evidence of it. Bill was one of two earthlings that spoke English. The Aliens triggered that same language module in the larger group. One of the humans at the meeting asked the Alien guide it they, the participants, could access this part of the human brain on their own once they returned to Earth and back into their own bodies. The Alien told them they could not. It was not a language currently spoken on earth, although that language did exist on Earth thousands of years ago.

Those from earth who were like Bill were not there to share with each other what they did back on Earth concerning secret programs. The intention of that particular visit was to broaden awareness among the members, and to learn a little more of what is involved in being a human in the galaxy. Bill, as did some of the others from earth, expressed their feelings to the Aliens that much was shown to them, but little was given to them to understand. The Aliens responded that not only do many levels of Aliens exist, but also many levels of human awareness exist in the human physical realm. The understanding that any one human achieves during his or her life depends on the level he or she is at. That alone, determines what they can comprehend, and keep for themselves when they leave and return to their planets. On Earth, there are seven levels of awareness. On other planets, the range was in the hundreds of levels. The level any person achieved did not correspond to intelligence alone, the condition of the soul had more to do with it. It was not for the Aliens to elaborate on what that mysterious substance was. It was something each individual needed to figure out on his or her own.

Two out of the twelve humans at the convention were at level seven. Bill was not one of them. The rest had achieved the rank of level five or six. Who was at what level remained hidden. Humans would only know their level after they had expired and moved up to a higher plane of existence. That was all that the Aliens would reveal concerning the soul. After returning to Earth, it was unlikely that Bill would see or meet any of the eleven people again. Throughout history, Aliens recruited humans to do work for them. Bill and the others were recent members of that fraternity.

One of the things revealed to Bill at the convention was that not all Aliens are benevolent. Some Aliens are evil and spend their time interfering with humanity. Bill learned that the ship he and the committee had in their possession involved a dispute between two Alien factions, and that the ship sustained damage because of that disagreement. The shipwreck could have been cleaned up with all signs of its existence hidden by the Aliens, but they where directed by others at a higher level of the matrix to leave it. The Aliens allowed it to come into the hands of certain chosen humans for the purpose of accelerating technological seeding onto the planet after the two World Wars. It also served to give the renegade Aliens the appearance of a small victory since they were determined to give the Earth a sampling of the "Alien terror" that loomed before Mankind. The Aliens let Bill know that such renegades made up a segment of the Alien population that was exiled on Earth eons ago. The renegade Aliens are a designed contravention in the Solar System—with a malicious disposition towards humans!

Lightning Source UK Ltd.
Milton Keynes UK
09 October 2009

144715UK00001B/214/P